The Cello

I was me. My feelings were mine and mine alone. I might hide them, file off the rough edges, form words and thoughts to explain them. But I couldn't alter them. For good or for bad I was stuck in this mind and body.

Life is difficult for Tom, living on a tough council estate with his mother; he has always felt different, somehow, from the other boys, and can't understand why. Is it just his love of classical music, and playing the cello, instead of the thumping, loud rock played by his friends that sets him apart? The arrival at school of Sanjeev, and his declaration of love, makes Tom realize the possibility that he might be gay.

And then the life of the estate is torn apart by angry demonstrations against paedophiles, Tom's cello teacher is assaulted, and in the confusion and bitterness that follows Tom himself is threatened. But to Tom music is his life and playing the cello is the one thing that gives his life meaning. His determination to carry on playing gives him the strength to stand up to the bullies and the bigots, and also to come to terms with his sexuality and what it will mean for the future.

James Riordan was born in Portsmouth and grew up there during the war. After school he had various jobs before doing his National Service in the RAF. After demobilization he gained degrees from Birmingham, London, and Moscow, then worked as a translator in Moscow. Back in England he lectured at Portsmouth Polytechnic and Birmingham and Bradford universities and, from 1989, at Surrey University where he was Professor of Russian Studies. He has written over twenty academic books, several collections of folk-tales, and a number of picture books. His first novel for children, *Sweet Clarinet*, won the 1999 NASEN Award and was shortlisted for the Whitbread Children's Book Award. *The Cello* is his sixth novel for Oxford University Press.

The Cello

Other Oxford books by James Riordan

The Cello

James Riordan

OXFORD
UNIVERSITY PRESS

OXFORD

UNIVERSITY PRESS

Great Clarendon Street, Oxford OX2 6DP

Oxford University Press is a department of the University of Oxford.
It furthers the University's objective of excellence in research, scholarship,
and education by publishing worldwide in

Oxford New York

Auckland Bangkok Buenos Aires
Cape Town Chennai Dar es Salaam Delhi Hong Kong Istanbul
Karachi Kolkata Kuala Lumpur Madrid Melbourne Mexico City Mumbai
Nairobi São Paulo Shanghai Singapore Taipei Tokyo Toronto

With an associated company in Berlin

Oxford is a registered trade mark of Oxford University Press
in the UK and in certain other countries

British Library Cataloguing in Publication Data available

ISBN 0 19 271913 0

1 3 5 7 9 10 8 6 4 2

Typeset by AFS Image Setters Ltd, Glasgow

Printed and bound in Great Britain by
Mackays of Chatham plc, Chatham, Kent

For David and Berni

Age Seven

Paddy was a weirdo.

You only had to shout 'Cats!' and he'd fly down the garden, barking his head off. But that wasn't all.

Whenever I took him for a walk, he'd show me up by sniffing other dogs. Just a sniff-sniff, snuffle-snuffle. Perfectly normal for dogs, you'd think. Mrs Figgins didn't think so.

She seemed to time her walkies to coincide with Paddy's. And since he was a big shaggy sheepdog and hers was one of those yappy little terriers, his attentions upset her.

'Keep that nasty brute in check!' she'd yell—on good days.

On bad days, it was 'Control his filthy habits or have him put down!'

At the time I used to think 'put down' meant down in the gutter, doing his business. Once I replied innocently, waving a hand behind me, 'He's already done it, down there, Mrs Figgins.'

Since it was her pavement edge where he'd deposited a pile of brown sausages, she wasn't best pleased.

That wasn't the only misunderstanding. One morning Paddy turned his attentions to Mr Jinxie while his mistress was chatting to Mum. Perhaps he got his smells mixed up because this time he didn't confine himself to a sniff. He tried to cock a leg over . . .

It was a bit like an elephant on a pushbike.

I did my best to pull him off, but not before the yappy tale-tit had whined to the Figgins woman.

1

Poor Paddy stood, head bowed, looking on guiltily as he got a lashing from her tongue.

'You filthy beast! You're either too dumb to know the difference or you're a canine pervert!'

At Mum's frantic hand signals, I swiftly made myself scarce, with Paddy yanking on the lead in a race for the park. Like our back garden, the park was his world of freedom, without humans tugging at the lead. He could sniff to his heart's content, bark, tiddle, have dogfights, even flirt with other dogs, male or female—Paddy wasn't choosy.

While I wandered after him, like a cowherd keeping a weather eye on Mother Nature, I thought over Mrs Figgins's words. What did she mean, 'he was too dumb to know the difference'? And what the heck was a 'canine pervert'?

Perhaps Paddy was from outer space and Mrs Figgins was his controller. Come to think of it, she did have a greeny-grey sheen about her. 'K-9 Purrvurt' . . . Was that his alien code?

Paddy didn't look any different from other mutts racing round the park, chasing their tails or sniffing bottoms. I'd have to ask Mum.

At tea-time I put it to her.

'What's a K-9 Purrvurt, Mum?'

She stared at me as if I was speaking Pekinese. Her slice of charred toast (Mum was on a diet—again) had halted before the pale lips. Then her mouth curled at the edges.

'You don't want to listen to Mrs Figgins. She wasn't serious.'

'What'd she mean, though?'

The good thing about Mum was that she always explained life's mysteries. Why there's famine in Africa. Why earthquakes happen. Whether there are ghosts, fairies, or a god. How some kids have freckles and ginger hair . . .

Perhaps that was because she had no one else to talk to. Since Dad left there were just the two of us.

She gazed into my earnest face and laughed.

'You're a funny little boy,' she said. 'Canine means dog, just as feline means cat. As for pervert, that's someone who does something unnatural.'

'Such as?' I persisted.

'Well, I suppose Mrs Figgins meant a male dog fancying another male dog.'

Apart from size difference, that seemed quite natural to me.

Mum put on her dead serious face.

'Perverts are dangerous. They hang around young kids—at playgrounds or schools—offering sweets or money to get them into cars.'

Her tone grew shrill and loud.

'Tom, promise me you won't take sweets. Don't even talk to strangers. You could get yourself killed!'

I promised.

'Why do perverts do that?' I asked.

She sighed, unsure of her words.

'You see, some men are that way inclined. They have an urge to feel up young boys. Girls too. They're what we call paedophiles or perverts.'

Mum had gone red. So I left it there.

I didn't really understand. But there was a lot I didn't understand at seven.

Age Nine

My birthday was coming up.

'What's it to be?' asked Mum brightly. 'Burgers and fries at McDonald's? Or Big Mac takeaways at No. 46?'

In my book birthdays are for Mums and Dads. I didn't want to spoil her fun, though.

'What do *you* fancy, Mum?' I asked.

'It's *your* big day, Tom,' she said. '*You* choose. You're only nine once.'

Once is enough, if you ask me. Christmas is barely bearable: a few naff presents, school holidays, Mum's rosy cheeks and laughing eyes over Christmas dinner. But then there are Gran and Grandad, Uncle Bob's unfunny jokes, Auntie Di, and . . . my cousin Harriet.

As I say, 'barely bearable'. But a birthday three weeks after Christmas is decidedly not cool. Mum should have been more careful.

Since Mum was broke, we stayed at home. Uncle Bob would organize a disco for me and my friends; he did that every Friday down at the local pub. Mum insisted on a mixed party: three girls, three boys. On top of that Auntie Di would bring Harriet—she was a year older than me and a pain.

The 'big day' arrived.

Mum had done me proud. Apart from my present—a mountain bike—she'd prepared a great 'mac-spread': big Macs and fries, milkshakes and Coke, cheeseburgers and chicken nuggets. That met all tastes. Almost.

Not Harriet's! One look at the table and she yelled, 'Yuck! I don't eat meat. I'm a veggie.'

4

That didn't stop her from stuffing herself with beef flavour crisps and hot sausage rolls.

Uncle Bob had rigged out our front room with black blinds and flashing strobe lights. And he had some fun discs.

Despite Mum's urging, we divided up—girls taking up most of the room, boys in one corner, with Mum slipping between the two groups. Of course, Harriet had to be the centre of attention, clearing a space for herself in the middle of the room and barging into everyone.

She wore trendy gear: black tights and a glitzy top that sparkled in the dark; her skinny shoulders and midriff were bare. Being a girl and old enough to make double figures, I guess she thought she looked sexy. You could tell by the way she thrust out her goosebumps under the skimpy top.

Some time during the disco I had to dodge out for the upstairs loo. I found poor Paddy sheltering under the basin, covering his ears with his paws. Disco music was obviously not his scene.

I zipped up, turned off the light, and was about to dash downstairs when a voice from the shadows scared the living daylights out of me.

'Here's your birthday present, Tommy.'

Despite the darkness, I knew who it was right away.

'Oh, you didn't half make me jump,' I said. 'Yeah, er . . . thanks.'

How stupid can you get!

On our upstairs landing she put her clammy arms round me, pushed her goosebumps into my chest and fumbled with her nose for my mouth.

I was well and truly zapped. I stood as rigid as a gravestone.

'Nine years old and never been kissed,' she breathed in my ear.

5

Now, I don't know how it feels to be crushed by an anaconda, or drown at the bottom of the sea, or have a knife held to your throat. But it couldn't be worse.

Harriet was bigger and stronger than me. She held me in an iron grip. Her pickled onion breath was clogging my nostrils. And her slimy lips were edging closer and closer to my clamped-shut mouth.

I couldn't shout 'Rape!' for fear of opening my lips. I could hardly knee her in the groin, as I might a boy. And I didn't have the strength to break free of her octopus arms . . .

What was I to do?

Rescue came from an unexpected quarter. K-9!

Perhaps he sensed his master was in mortal danger. Whatever his doggy instincts, it worked a treat. A snap at an ankle.

Harriet let out a shriek. Her arms unwound and she hobbled down the stairs, screaming blue murder.

Naturally, her cries emptied the disco floor; they all came crowding into the hallway. The females looked from poor Harriet up to me in horror and disgust, the boys in surprise and awe.

It certainly put the lid on my birthday party. Auntie Di took her injured girl home amid dark mutterings of 'sex fiend' and, to Mum, 'You want to keep him on a leash!' Harriet kept her mouth shut, and my protests cut no ice with my new enemies (the girls) and admirers (the boys).

First off, even Mum sided with her weeping niece. She was a bit taken aback, of course: 'How could you, Tom?' But when I gave my version she began to waver.

'Mum, she went and grabbed me in the dark.'

Stony face. I tried again.

'I don't even like girls.'

Even stonier. I was getting desperate.

'Right, tell me this, then,' I shouted. 'How could I have ripped a hole in her tights and bitten her ankle?'

That had her. But it was Paddy's doleful look, those big brown guilty eyes that clinched it.

One thing's for sure.

It put me off kissing girls for good.

Age Ten

In my class at school we had this boy, David. A clumsier clown you can't imagine. You know how some boys grow too fast for their bodies; their head, arms, and legs can't keep up. And this wobbly lump was forever bumping into tables, knocking over chairs, upsetting paint and flower pots.

Boys like him often become bullies. It doesn't take them long to suss that other kids are scared or want them as mates. If you tackle them at football, they just flatten you, like a steamroller.

Not David. Just the opposite. Other kids bullied *him*.

As soon as they twigged he was a big softy, they made his life a misery. They were always trying to get him into trouble—hiding his school bag, tossing his trainers on the roof or in the school pond, kicking his shins under the table. Once, on his way to school, some boys pinched his dinner money and brand new Playstation.

That wasn't all. Both boys and girls would call him names: 'Cissy', 'Cry-baby', 'Fatty'. In the playground they'd dance round him chanting, 'David is a poofter! David is a poofter!'

Him being bigger, I guess, gave them a sense of power. David versus Goliath, except that David *was* Goliath! They'd only stop teasing when he started crying. Then, having got what they wanted, they'd run off laughing.

Even though he was big and awkward, David was the gentlest, kindest boy in school. If anyone needed help with school work or wanted to borrow a ruler or pencil, David would oblige instantly. If Miss wanted someone to sit with a sick child, she knew she could rely on him.

And he was so artistic. When explaining something, his hands would flutter in the air like doves. When reciting a verse, his tongue would taste the flavour as if it were a sweet.

If you cared to listen you'd sit there spellbound, carried away on a magic carpet of fantasy—'to the land where the Bong-tree grows. And there in a wood a Piggy-wig stood, with a ring at the end of his nose.'

He was especially good at mimicking, he'd get right into the character, particularly witches and fairies: 'You are welcome, most noble Sorceress, to the land of the Munchkins. We are so grateful to you for having killed the Wicked Witch of the East, and for setting our people free.'

Real scary. As if he was there, in the Land of Oz.

Trouble is, there are kids who *never* listen. Kids who hate anyone who works hard, hands in homework on time, is neat and tidy, someone who puts his heart into poetry. Such spoilsports think it cool to humiliate those they call 'teacher's pet'.

It's a shame. If only they'd let themselves listen and learn. They'd be inspired by David's ability to bring words to life. But, oh no, they couldn't wait to take the mickey. All bullies are cowards, and one such idiot coined the nickname 'Dorothy', from David's favourite story, *The Wizard of Oz*.

And it stuck. From then on, even among the girls, David was 'Dorothy', spoken with a snigger and fake American accent.

Though I didn't want to be picked on, I took every opportunity to help David, show him I was on his side. At first he was wary, thinking I was trying to trap him; but it wasn't long before we became the best of friends.

The better I got to know him, the more fond I grew.

Like me, he was an only child. But whereas Mum was bringing me up, he was at home with his dad. Although he didn't like speaking about it, I found out later that his mum had left them for a car salesman. His dad only owned a rusty old bike; I suppose his mum wanted to travel in comfort.

He never invited me to his place, even though it was only two streets away on the estate. It was as if some dark secret lurked behind his front door. So I never did get to see his dad. I wasn't to know there was another reason for his mother leaving home.

Much later I discovered that David's dad liked dressing up in women's clothing—tights, high heels, false boobs, the lot. No wonder he didn't want anyone to bump into his old man.

But David would regularly come to our house. I think he liked Mum making a fuss of him. He was always more at ease with women than with men. Inevitably, I got stick from other boys, especially the football team. In the changing room they'd act all coy about undressing in front of me; and they'd ask after my 'boyfriend'.

Still, since they relied on my goal-keeping skills, they knew not to push me too far. In any case, there was nothing namby-pamby about me.

All of a sudden, however, David vanished.

One day he was at school, the next he wasn't. Teachers, kids, dinner ladies . . . no one knew his whereabouts. I didn't like to go knocking on his door, what with his dad being hostile.

So I remained in the dark. Of course, the school scandal-mongers had their own versions. 'A paedophile ring had done him in.'

'A fat sugar daddy had taken him off on his yacht.'

'They'd found he was really a girl and sent him to an exclusive girls' school.'

Whatever the truth, I missed him. I shed a few tears into my pillow for the first few nights.

It was about six months later that Mum heard the story on the grapevine: from a friend of a friend of a friend . . . We were sitting at breakfast one Saturday morning when she looked up from the paper and said casually, 'By the way, you remember your friend David?'

''Course I do!' I said, eager for news.

'He got transferred to another school,' she muttered. 'When he was better . . . '

'Better? Mum-mm!'

She saw there was no escape. Putting the paper down and taking a sip of her coffee, she managed to get it out. In a quiet voice, she said, 'He tried to top himself, son. The bullying was too much to bear. His dad found him in the nick of time, hanging from his bedroom door.'

She let her words sink in, like raindrops in a dust-dry soil. I must have gone as white as a sheet, for she got up and put her arm round my shoulder. We were both crying by now.

Through her tears, she murmured, 'I had a phone call last night from David's father. He said his son was fine now, and wanted you to know how much your friendship meant to him. They both reckoned he should make a fresh start—new school, new district, new friends, cut himself off from the past.'

It was all too much. I ran to my room.

Why are kids so cruel?

Age Ten and a Half

Mum was mad about music. Not just pop tunes. She'd switch from pop to classical all the time: one minute she'd be tapping her foot and singing away, the next she'd have a dreamy look in her eyes and be waving her arms in the air as if conducting an orchestra.

'It's in the blood,' she'd say.

She blamed it on her Irish roots. Mind you, there was a lot she blamed on the Irish: her red hair, her romantic nature, her way with words, her fiery temper (her 'paddy' she called it), even her weakness for the whiskey 'comforter'.

'If it's in your nature there's nothing you can do about it,' she'd insist.

I thought a lot about that. What was *my* nature?

I was me. My feelings were mine and mine alone. I might hide them, file off the rough edges, form words and thoughts to explain them. But I couldn't alter them. For good or for bad I was stuck in this mind and body.

One day I drew up a list.

TOM GOODALL'S NATURE

Pluses	Minuses
Kind and generous	Too soft
Tough, macho man	Stubborn, pig-headed
Sensitive	Cry too easily
Good at writing	Poor at art and maths
Helpful, eager to please	Show-off
Hard-working	Definitely *not* clever
Creative	Scruffy, untidy

That wasn't really the end of my list; it could have gone on and on. But it set me thinking about other feelings I had, deep inside me. Although they kept popping up, I quickly pushed them down again. Partly because I felt unable to understand them—maybe I didn't *want* to. And partly because I thought I'd grow out of them.

It was as if they weren't part of me, my nature, like the items on my list. So I told myself I'd deal with them later, when I was old enough to understand.

Mum must have come across my scribbled list. Because one day at breakfast, she said, 'You've your father in you.'

'Why's that, Mum?'

Since Dad had moved out when I was four, and had never been in touch from that day to this, I never really knew him. I could barely remember what he looked like, apart from a moustache. Anyway, Mum wouldn't talk about him, as if he'd never touched her life.

So I didn't know what she was on about.

'He was as stubborn as you, and a show-off.'

The penny dropped.

'Oh, that's not fair,' I cried. 'That's personal.'

'Well,' she said defensively, 'you shouldn't leave it about. I thought it was a shopping list.'

Mention of Dad gave me an opening.

'Didn't Dad give me anything nice?'

She smiled quickly with her mouth, but not her eyes. He would never be forgiven in our house.

'Football,' she said dismissively. 'That's all he was good for.'

Her smouldering eyes told me it was time to change the subject.

'Since you know all about me,' I said with a grin, 'what do you think? Did I leave anything out?'

She smiled with her green eyes this time.

'What do *you* think? Only *you* know how you feel.'

I'd like to have told her about the deep-down worries. But I didn't dare. Likely as not, they were just growing pains; I'd grow out of them. So they weren't worth mentioning.

'Well,' I said slowly, 'I'm too modest to admit to being Mum's good-looking, helpful son.'

She laughed and started to sing.

'Someday I'll wish upon a star
And wake up where the clouds are far behind me,
Where troubles melt like lemon drops,
Away above the chimney tops
That's where you'll find me.

Somewhere over the rainbow skies are blue,
And the dreams that you dare to dream
Really do come true . . . '

She came round the table and gave me a great big hug.

Age Eleven and a Quarter

As I said, Mum loved music. It ran in her family. Grandad played the violin, Gran the piano. Gran's dad had played cornet in the Irish Guards, while her mum had played the church organ. Grandad used to say that when they were young they had to make their own entertainment; there was no telly in those days.

As a girl, Mum had worked her way up from tin whistle to recorder to flute. She even had grade certificates to show for it; and a big cardboard photo of a girl in pigtails playing in the city orchestra.

Once she started going out with Dad, though, she packed it in. On his orders. It didn't fit his image of a girlfriend.

Now and again, when I came home from school, I'd catch her at it: sitting at the kitchen table, warbling away on her flute. It sounded wonderful. Yet the moment she saw me, she'd jump up and put the flute back in the cupboard—as if I'd caught her eating chocolate biscuits.

'That's past,' she'd say, all red and flustered. 'I only play for me, to cheer meself up.'

No matter how hard I begged, she'd never give way. Real pig-headed she was sometimes. I knew whom I'd got my stubbornness from. All the same, as a special treat, she took me to a concert at the Guildhall.

Now, on our council estate, you kept quiet about that sort of 'music'. Apart from TV jingles, the wonderful world of classical music was a foreign land, music for 'toffs'. *Our* music was always loud, drowning in *thump-THUMP-**THUMP!***

Up till now Mum had kept her guilty 'music' secret to herself. But at the Guildhall, she was in for a shock. During the interval we were standing around in the foyer when someone called Mum's name.

'Jeanette. It is Jeanette, isn't it?'

A tall man, rosy-cheeked, with fluffy grey hair was coming towards us, a big smile creasing his ruddy face. Even for concert-goers he was dressed oddly. Not posh, in black suit and tie, but in powder-blue jeans, red sweater, and flowery silk neckerchief.

Mum looked a bit awkward.

'Oh, hello, Terry,' she said. 'Long time no see. This is my son, Tom.'

Terry beamed down at me, leant forward and shook my hand.

'Hi, Tom. Ooh, I say, are you musical, like your mum? She's fab.'

'*Was* musical,' said Mum quickly. 'And *never* fab.'

Turning to me, she completed the introductions.

'Tom, this is Mr Wimbush. He was the brains behind the City Orchestra—conductor, leader, arranger, big brother to us all.'

Mr Wimbush disagreed.

'I was just the dogsbody. Your mother was the star,' he said. 'She could have gone on to a professional career.'

Well, well. I looked at Mum in a new light. The only professionals I knew played football. So she was *that* good, eh? Star quality. My mum!

Just then the buzzer sounded: the second half was about to start.

Before he bustled off, Mr Wimbush thrust a card into Mum's hand.

'Darling, do keep in touch,' he said. 'Maybe I can help the boy. Toodle-oo. Enjoy Elgar.'

Mum nodded and, without glancing at the card, popped it into her purse.

'Bye.'

Back in our Circle seats, we watched the orchestra take their places on the big stage; we politely clapped the conductor, a silver-haired Dutchman, and, a few moments later, clapped again as a shy young woman walked to centre stage. She was carrying what looked like a big violin.

She took her seat in front of the orchestra and, instead of putting the instrument under her chin, she wedged it between her knees. Then, she nodded to the conductor. The poor girl looked ever so nervous, wiping her hands on a hanky and flicking back her long dark hair.

The moment she started playing, though, she was transformed. Her lips pressed tight, eyes half closed, head swaying to and fro, hair flying. Such energy, such passion, such beauty.

At the end, she sat back, drained and glowing with sweat. Once again she was a shy young girl. Yet as radiant as the smiling moon.

There was the briefest of silences—you could have heard a crisp crack. Then the dam burst: the audience clapped, stamped, and shouted, 'Bravo! Bravo!' She walked quickly from the stage, but had to return three times before disappearing, head bowed.

I turned to Mum, but couldn't speak for choking on my feelings. Mum's cheeks were wet with tears. We walked together in silence, down the steps, out into the dark night. Only on the bus did I find my voice.

'Mum, what was that big violin she played?'

Mum sighed, then spoke hoarsely, 'It isn't a violin; it's a violoncello, better known as cello. Did you like it?'

'It was ace,' I said quietly. 'Wish I could play.'

'You will, son,' she promised. 'One day you will.'

Age Eleven and Three Quarters

Mum took me to two more concerts. Good, but not as moving as the cello concerto. On our second visit, she left me for a brief chat with her old friend Terry. He was holding forth, laughing loudly, surrounded by three or four admiring women. Quite a ladies' man.

Was he one of Mum's old boyfriends? She seemed pretty fond of him. I really ought to put another plus and minus on my character list:

Loyalty to Mum   Jealousy of boyfriends

Not that she had any boyfriends, old or new. 'You're my one and only boyfriend,' she used to tell me. I guess the upset over Dad put her off men. All the same, I couldn't help feeling jealous if some outsider ever paid her attention. And this Mr Wimbush was all over her, kissing her on both cheeks, putting his arm round her shoulders, thrusting his red face into hers. Yuck!

I felt like going over and pulling her away, telling him she belonged to me. Her first words made me feel worse.

'We're going to see more of Mr Wimbush. He only lives on East Lawn Way.'

East Lawn Way! That's where Harriet lived, a tidy walk from our place. But too close for comfort.

Thoughts of me coming home from school and catching them at it spoiled the start of the Brahms after the interval. But it didn't last long. That's the great thing about music. It has the power to cheer you up, no matter how miserable you feel. It floods your mind and flushes out all the garbage.

By the end of the concert I'd forgotten all about the

touchy-feely Mr Wimbush. We rode home in silence, lost in our own thoughts. But once home Mum went and spoiled it all.

'Tom,' she said over our hot chocolate, 'you remember what I said about the cello. I've some good news. Mr Wimbush says he'll take you on.'

Oh, so that was his game. I saw through it at once; getting to her through me. I wasn't one to sulk. Best out with it.

'Do you fancy him, Mum?'

She stared at me as if I'd caused a nasty smell. Then, putting a finger to her cheek—giving my question serious consideration—she said slowly, 'I don't *fancy* him. I'm fond of Terry. A kinder, more sensitive man would be hard to find. I owe a lot to him. No one knows more about music than Terry; he lives and breathes it.'

'Was he your boyfriend?'

My question hit her like a slap in the face. She looked shocked.

'Wha-at? *Terry!*'

To my surprise, her drawn face suddenly collapsed into squiggles and creases as she burst out laughing. Then, just as abruptly, noticing my hurt scowl, she grew serious. She must have guessed.

'Tommy! You're jealous! Sweet. I'm glad somebody loves me. But you and I need a firm talk about the birds and the bees.'

Whatever did she mean? I studied the lacework brown pattern left by my chocolate drink.

'First of all,' said Mum, 'Mr Wimbush is old enough to be my father. A lovely, lovely man, but too old even for a lady of my mature years.'

She paused, her eyes and fingers on her black concert skirt. When she spoke it was in hushed tones as if the neighbours might hear.

'Second, well, Terry adores women's company. But he doesn't go out with them—if you know what I mean.'

I didn't. Well, not exactly. And here was a chance to learn more. So acting dumb, I said, 'What *do* you mean, Mum?'

There was no running away. So she came right out with it.

'Terry's gay. That's how he was born: the genes sometimes get mixed up. I guess it's a bit like a girl growing up in a boy's body, or the other way round.'

I thought that over. It wasn't easy to take in. Of course, I knew about gays; lesbians too. That sort of stuff was on telly all the time, and in the papers. Men dressing up as women and acting daft, famous gay men dying of AIDs, pop singers 'coming out', like the lad from that Irish boyband.

But in the real world, at school, teachers never mentioned it, and kids sniggered at the very word 'gay'. Except they never called it that. They took the mickey out of 'queers', 'poofters', 'shirt-lifters', that sort of thing.

'I suppose your friend David was like that,' continued Mum, seeing my confusion. 'Sad, really, there's so much ignorance about. It isn't easy being gay.'

I thought of David: the taunts, the bullying, what he must have gone through. No wonder he attempted suicide, then tried to escape by moving school. And I thought of Mr Wimbush. Yet he seemed such a happy, carefree soul.

Come to think of it, there *was* something they had in common. They both spoke a bit girly, acted a bit cissy, what boys at school called 'poncy'. That night in bed I thought it over.

I definitely didn't speak poncy. There was nothing girly

about me. I wasn't into poetry; I played football. I didn't much like girls' company; I went around with the lads. I spoke in a boy's voice. (Note: I must try to cultivate a low, husky voice.)

Thank God I wasn't gay!

Age Thirteen

I'd been learning the cello for over a year, and was just beginning to bash out some decent tunes. Well, let's say slightly more tuneful than my initial squeaks and burps. Mr Wimbush was a natural-born teacher: patient, inventive, full of enthusiasm. Mum was right about him being generous.

The battered old cello was his pride and joy. You could see that by the way he hugged and patted it, like a pet dog. He'd had it since a boy—a present from his mother on his tenth birthday. And he'd won prizes with it—at county level. He'd even once played a solo piece at the Albert Hall up in The Smoke.

Yet he gave it to me.

'No use to me any more, Tom,' he said with a sigh. 'My fingers are all stiff and bent, full of the old arthritis. It gives me grief just to see it gathering dust.'

He exaggerated. To inspire me, he'd pick up the bow and caress the most wonderful music out of the instrument. One of his favourites was 'The Birds'; he made the music sound soft and mellow as the birds were resting, then the notes fluttered up, soaring and dipping in the sky. Beautiful.

But there were times he'd suddenly break off with a string of old-fashioned words.

'Oh, blinkin' Jiminy Cricket! Darn and dash and damn!'

His favourite was 'Oh, cockalorum!'

He'd get so cross with himself, it was funny to watch. He'd talk angrily to his fingers, telling them off for not doing what he told them. One time he blamed his stiff fingers on 'playing with himself' too much. I wasn't sure it meant what I thought it meant. Surely, grown-ups didn't do that sort of thing? Anyway, I went and put my foot in it by asking.

He gave one of his characteristic laughs, like a horse whinnying.

'Sorry, Tom. That's rude. I shouldn't have said it. Comes with living by myself too long,' he said, excusing himself.

To change the subject, I asked, 'Have you always lived alone, Mr Wimbush?'

He gave me an odd look, perhaps wondering whether Mum had let me into his dark secret.

'Ye-e-s,' he said. Then he added with a sigh, 'It can get a teeny-weeny bit lonely sometimes.'

'But you've loads of friends, haven't you?' I said.

''S not really the same. Not like living with someone . . . Someone to come home to, tell your troubles to, trust and love.'

'Have you ever loved anyone?'

It just popped out. I regretted it the moment I heard it out loud. None of my business. But he didn't take offence. He just smiled mysteriously, and a trifle sadly.

His clear blue eyes looked at me uncertainly, perhaps wondering whether to spin me a yarn about old girlfriends, failed relationships, being left on the shelf . . . Finally, he coughed nervously and said quietly, 'Yes, I have. Twice. But it didn't work out.'

I bit my tongue. This time I wouldn't pry. That doesn't mean to say my expression wasn't asking questions. I could see he was caught in two minds: whether to cover up or come out with it.

Of course, he didn't know that I knew he was gay.

Then it suddenly tumbled out.

'Yes, they were both sailors. Daft really. They were always at sea. I only saw them in port occasionally. Not the best of circumstances for a stable relationship.'

I wasn't sure what he meant. But he'd shared his secret with me. And I felt grateful. No more questions. I could see from his flushed face and sad eyes that it hurt him to talk about it, especially to a young boy.

All at once he looked up and said with a cheeky grin, 'How about you, Tom? Going steady? Fallen in love yet?'

I was itching to tell him about my mixed-up feelings, to ask his advice. I felt I could talk about things with him that I wouldn't dare with Mum. With her I was always worried about hurting her. Or saying something she wouldn't understand. She was a woman, after all!

But the time wasn't right. Maybe later.

'I'm too young for that,' I said. 'In any case, what with cello and football I've no time for girls.'

Then I added with a nervous smile, 'Or boys for that matter.'

He gave me a quizzical look, then giggled.

'Good for you. Don't let love get in the way of football. As for music, that's no replacement for love. It is its complement, its expression; it *is* love, but in another form. *"If music be the food of love, play on, Give me excess of it . . . O spirit of love, how quick and fresh art thou."* William Shakespeare. He knew a bit about love and music.' Then he added with a twinkle in his eye, 'The good thing about music is that it has no mistress *or* master.'

Harriet Again!

The only problem with playing the cello is practice. To practise I had to sit in my room with the instrument between my knees and my music propped on a metal music stand. That meant lugging the canvas bag all through the streets from my house to Mr Wimbush's and back.

Now a cello isn't a pair of football boots, a skateboard, or scooter. And our district isn't exactly a des. res. area, with a Mercedes or BMW parked outside every other door.

Once a week I had to run the gauntlet of the mickey-takers. As I say, the cello isn't a pair of football boots. It's big, too big to be passed off as a guitar. So I had to put up with jeers and cat-calls, particularly at school.

'Here comes Mr Tambourine Man!' was the kindest remark. Since few of my school pals had ever heard of, let alone seen, a cello, the invisible body in the canvas bag gave them the most fanciful ideas:

'The goalie's carrying his own goal-posts around!'

'Dr Strangelove and his body parts!'

Once they discovered that my 'bag of bones' was being taken to the 'queer's place', their minds ran riot. It was my dear cousin Harriet who let everyone into the secret of my music lessons—and of Mr Wimbush. She it was who led the chants one spring morning in the school yard.

> 'Tomm-ee . . . likes it up the arse,
> Tomm-ee . . . likes it up the arse!'

And so on for six more boring verses.

How cool! I suppose I should have turned a deaf ear. After all, she'd never forgiven me for old Paddy's 'love bite'.

But there's a difference between having a laugh at someone, and being downright nasty. And she'd crossed that line. If I didn't do something right away, the mud could stick and I'd be labelled a 'shirt-lifter'.

So I marched over to the 'cheerleader' by the bike shed, intending to murder her in cold blood. The only trouble was she was older and bigger than me, and I wasn't into belting girls. All the same, I couldn't let her get away with it.

'You should know, you slag,' I yelled in her face. 'That's where you take it!'

Harriet never could take a joke. What made it worse was her friends turning on her, supported by my football team-mates.

'Harr—ee—et . . . likes it up the arse . . . '

She lost her cool. Out came her sharp claws, like a wildcat. If it hadn't been for the duty teacher, she'd have turned my face into Southampton's colours—red-and-white stripes!

We both got an hour's detention after school.

And once again I had to answer to Mum for offending Auntie Di's precious pearl.

'Harriet says you used filthy language about her in school,' said Mum in an ominously quiet voice. 'I want to know what you said.'

Oh dear. Mum didn't permit bad language in the house. To utter rude words to Mum was more than my life was worth. I stalled.

'But, Mum . . . I only said what she shouted at me, in front of everyone. I didn't lay a finger on her, honest. It was her who went to attack me.'

'What did you say?!'

'I can't tell you,' I said miserably. 'It's too rude. Anyway, I didn't mean it. She got up my nose and I flung her own words back at her.'

'All right, if you won't tell me, I'll ask your Auntie Diana and the school.'

I was caught. If Harriet gave her version, I'd get it in the neck. If the duty teacher had heard anything, it was only what I'd said back. Either way, my goose was well and truly cooked.

'Come on, out with it,' said Mum sternly.

'You won't like it, Mum,' I said, still playing for time. 'Well, when I got to school, she and some of her mates started calling me names, saying I liked it . . . er, sorry, up my bottom . . . '

'Why should she say that?' asked Mum, eyes narrowing, clearly shocked.

'Oh-h, apparently because I go for cello lessons to Mr Wimbush and, well, you know, some kids call him names since he's a bit, you know, cissyish.'

Suddenly she caught on. Her face went pale, as if she blamed herself. Then she exploded into one of her 'paddies', breaking her own house rules.

'Bastards! What d'you expect from ignorant peasants on this estate? They've nothing else to do, nothing to fill their boring, miserable lives with. So they snigger at people who are different. Why can't they leave them alone? One moment it's "Pakis", the next it's "immigrants", then it's homosexuals . . . Hateful, bigoted, nasty . . . Ugh! Words fail me . . . '

With any luck Mum's rage would make her forget all about my part in the name-calling. But when the storm had blown itself out, she looked hard at me, as if suddenly remembering something.

'How is it *you* got detention?'

I could hardly keep up the 'poor innocent victim' act,

since she'd find out anyway. So, head bent, I confessed to my guilt.

'I'm sorry, Mum. But I lost my temper—you know my Irish roots—and I went and called her a slag.'

'What else?' she said, giving me a piercing green-eyed stare, making no allowance for my Irish roots.

'I threw her words back at her, saying that's where she liked it.'

'I see,' said Mum. She hissed like a snake, recoiling into her armchair. 'I see . . . '

She didn't tell me what she saw. At least not then.

That was that.

Kids at school found someone else to poke fun at; and the heat was turned off me . . . and Harriet.

Music Club

Shortly after my detention, word got round school that I was musical. Now, music was one of the few subjects on which staff and students saw eye to eye. Reading, writing, maths, art—they were naff.

That's not to say that all kids had an attitude problem. Some were really talented and dead interested in stories and poems, drawing, stats. But the fact that they were *praised* by teachers was enough to set them apart—like Jews and Muslims sitting out assembly.

And no one liked being different. The bullies picked on you, singled you out as being on *the other side*. They'd make it their self-appointed mission to sort you out. Either you saw things their way or you suffered. The choice was yours . . .

Music, though, was neutral ground. Quite a few kids fancied themselves as singers, guitar strummers, drum bangers. In their dreams they saw their future careers in show business, making millions, appearing on telly. After all, most pop stars spoke as they did, came from rough estates and beat-up schools.

So our Music Club was thriving. A lot of members attended after school, even practised in the lunch break. And although some dropped out after giving it a try, many stayed on, working hard at whatever talent they had—or *might have* if only they worked hard enough.

So popular was the Music Club that it had three sections.

1. A steel band, about forty strong, with a long waiting

list. Though they played calypso music, there wasn't a black face among them.

2. A pop workshop. This was the favourite. It was so popular that it had to be subdivided into vocals, keyboard, and other instruments. It also had a division of sound recordists and 'arrangers'.

3. String group. This was by far the smallest, made up of classical string instruments and padded out with teachers and outsiders—mainly governors and parents. Most of the school didn't even know of its existence. That didn't stop the Head referring to it as the 'School Orchestra'.

So when Head of Music called me in for a chat one lunchtime, the last thing on my mind was joining the 'School Orchestra'.

'Now then, young Goodall,' said Mr Stares, all bright and breezy. 'How do you fancy joining the Music Club?'

I was wary. Which branch exactly? Not vocals or oil-drummers, that's for sure.

'I don't think I can fit it in with all my other commitments,' I replied.

'What commitments?' he scoffed.

'Oh, uh, all the homework we get, playing football for school, helping out at home, my paper round. It's never ending, sir.'

'Do you like music?'

'Yeah, everybody does, don't they?'

We sparred about for a bit, with Mr Stares looking for an opening and me covering up. Then all at once he landed a blow below the belt. Oooff!

'You play cello with Mr Wimbush; and you've been spotted at the Guildhall.'

'Oh that, yeah, sure,' I said, caught off guard. 'But I'm no good. Honest, sir.'

'Let me be the judge of that. According to your tutor, you're very promising.'

I should've known you can't keep anything secret round our way. Evidently, school had rung up Mr Wimbush. What could he say? He didn't want to drop me in it, but he could hardly deny teaching me.

To cut a long story short, I got roped in. The 'orchestra' run by Mr Stares badly needed the one instrument they lacked: a cello. I was the missing link.

Next Tuesday, after my paper round, I found myself back in the school hall with my precious canvas bag. One rule Terry Wimbush had insisted on from the start was note-reading. So when Mr Stares gave out the music, I was able to follow the cello part.

If it had been a proper orchestra it mightn't have mattered. But this was less than football team size. The only other students, both girls, were violins. Besides them we had a double bass (Mr Stares), two violas, and two violins. So when I started bowing and scraping there was no one to smother the noise with a sound blanket.

Even so, I have to admit that playing in a group was very different from playing solo. You felt part of a team, encouraged by the playing of others—and their occasional fluffs. For the first time since I'd limped through a full cello exercise, I felt the thrill of making music. Despite everything, it sounded great.

I'd joined the group just at the right time! They were practising for the school concert, scheduled for a month's time. The Concert was all part of the school music programme, when the Music Club showed off its stuff before relatives, friends, and strangers from off the estate.

Although our school was rock bottom of the achievement league, and had the worst reputation in the city for violence, truancy, drugs, vandalism, that sort of thing, we stuffed all-comers at football and . . . we could knock out some good tunes.

So the city fathers (and a sprinkling of mothers) would turn up for our Music Club Concert, with a trail of reporters, governors, and even the odd talent scout (well, anyone who looked funky we reckoned was a talent scout!). I guess it was our chance to shout out: 'See what us no-hopers can do if we try!'

Our 'string band' was detailed to open and close the concert. 'Keep it short!' the Deputy Head had warned. 'We don't want to send them to sleep.' Poor Mr Stares— 'Upstairs' we called him—had come up with three string quartets, by Borodin, Vivaldi, and Tchaikovsky.

'Most of them won't know a quartet's only four anyway,' he grumbled. 'And twice as many of you can cover up the mistakes of the others.'

Since the whole idea of the Concert was to show off school talent, Mr Stares was pinning his hopes on a violin solo from Fiona Panis. Her parents had put her on the fiddle when she was five, so she was an 'old trouper'. Sometimes she was brilliant, sometimes awful.

'Fidgety Fee' we called her in class. She could never keep still, twitching and jumping at her own shadow. Put her in a room by herself and she'd make her violin sing like an angel. In public she was a quivering jelly.

Fiona was Big Risk. And Mr Stares knew it. After our second practice he called me back.

'Goodall, you may not be ''good-all'' the time. But you have talent, lad, talent.'

Ha-ha. 'Upstairs' can stare, while Goodall gives f . . . all!

Something nasty was brewing.

'I'm going to have a word with your tutor. See if we can squeeze a short solo out of you. It's either ''Panicky Panis'' or ''Goodnight Goodall'' by the look of things.'

No 'Would you like to perform all alone in front of a laughing, jeering mob of so-called schoolfriends?' I was just another brick in the wall, an item to fill a gap, just in case Fidgety Fee got stage fright.

That's how I came to join the 'school orchestra'. And that's how I came to make my solo debut after less than two years' practice. Scary or what?

'Yesterday'

I put in so much practice my finger tips grew hard pads where I kept pressing the cello strings. Luckily old Ma Figgins next door was as deaf as a doorpost. But from the non-stop yapping I must have driven her flea-bag terrier nuts. He was fortunate I hadn't taken up the trumpet.

Mr Wimbush was a crazy Beatles fan. So when we sat down to select my party piece, he suggested Lennon and McCartney's 'Yesterday'. I agreed, relieved it wasn't some Bach prelude and fugue. My mates would've been chuffed!

He went into town to buy the music and transcribed the whole lot for cello.

Is there a more beautiful song? Mellow and sad, just . . . well, lovely. I found myself humming, singing, whistling, even tapping it out with my fingers on the duvet in bed.

Mum was a great support. She even delivered my papers two evenings a week, so I could have more practice with Mr Wimbush. He was more excited than me—and very demanding. 'We've got to get it perfect,' he kept saying with sighs and tut-tut-tuts, 'Oh my, oh my, oh my!' and 'cockalorums', by the dozen.

Whenever I played he'd throw his head back, close his eyes, and move his lips with the tune. He'd memorize every note of the song and every note and pause of my playing. Then came the post-mortem.

'Much softer—*pianissimo*—at the start; hard: tap-tap-tap—*staccato*—there; rising, fly away, up, up, up—*forte*—in the middle eight bars. Back down the scale and into *crescendo* for the finale. Bravo! Bravissimo!'

He played the whole lot with his hands, face, and body, living the music, inspiring me all the while.

'Chiaroscuro ('kiaroscuro' he pronounced it)—that's the key, Tom. Light and shade, contrast, paint the music in picture colours. Greys and browns and mauves here, reds and blues and yellows there. So the audience can *see* the picture you're painting, *feel* the contrasts.'

Once or twice he attempted to play for me to hear what he meant. But by now his fingers were all gnarled, like twigs on an old apple tree. And he'd screw up his eyes in agony. Instead, he sang, hummed, tapped his foot, nodded and swayed, playing an invisible cello with body and soul.

Mr Stares wasn't at all keen on our choice of music. It made him turn his attention back to Fiddling Fee. But when she came out in red panic blotches all over her face and hands, he had to back down.

'I don't hold with souped-up pop tunes,' he said. 'Leave that to our pop stars who don't know their arpeggio from their elegy. But you and Wimbush leave me no choice.'

He muttered on about having to put up with amateur school kids in his 'orchestra'. All the same, after the next rehearsal he had grudgingly to admit it 'sounded OK'. Mind you, it was one thing playing before eight sympathetic fellow musicians; it'd be quite another on the night. I'd be on a well-lit stage, looking down on a darkened hall full of grinning baboons trying to take the piss.

It was bad enough in the run-up to the concert. To say my friends didn't appreciate the finer points of music is a whopping great understatement. As far as they were concerned, classical music was for snobs and weirdos; it was something to put in Room 101, down the chute with chess, hymn-singing, and trainspotting.

I might've agreed myself if it hadn't been for Mum

and Mr Wimbush. On the morning of the concert, I mentioned it to Mum.

'Why don't my friends like classical music?'

'Who says they don't?'

'Well, they're always poking fun. You know, ''Ballet's football for poofs!'', ''Opera's dead boring!'' '

'Have they ever seen it?'

'No, I s'ppose not.'

'Well, then, they don't know what they're missing, do they? Their lives would be so much richer if they went to concerts and art galleries.'

'That's not fair, Mum. Most of my friends have got no one to take them, encourage a love of music or art. You and Mr Wimbush aren't exactly typical round here, are you?'

Slowly she shook her head and gave a wry smile.

'No, and look where it's got me: all on my lonesome.'

'Come on, Mum. You've got *me*. Anyway, living alone has nothing to do with music.'

She brightened up.

'You're right, son. And who knows, you could show people what they're missing. I've done up your cello with furniture polish, and cleaned your shoes. You are *not* going to the concert in those trainers! And make sure your nails are clean.'

At lunchtime, we 'classical' instruments had to squeeze into the art room because the 'proper musicians' needed the hall and the steel band had bagged the gym. Not that it mattered. There were only five of us—a quintet; the rest were otherwise engaged.

We struggled through our 'orchestral' numbers, sounding very thin and drowned out by Mr Stares's double bass. It was like playing in a broom cupboard.

I was crap. Whether it was the slippery wood or my nerves I don't know. But if I performed like that in the evening, I'd put people off music for good.

'Thanks, Mum'

Mum did my paper round that evening while I had a last-minute run-through with Mr Wimbush. I told him of my disastrous 'dress rehearsal'.

'You naughty boy,' he said. 'Don't you dare let Jeanette and me down tonight. Now, listen. We *all* get butterflies. That's OK. It makes the adrenalin flow. What I used to tell your mum is what my mother told me. Before you start to play, sit back and seek out a face in the audience. Then play for that person alone. It helps you forget your nerves.'

It sounded simple.

By six thirty the hall was packed with mums, dads and stepdads, aunts and uncles, grans and grandads, as well as kids ranging from babes-in-arms to our old boys and girls. Even Harriet was there.

The front two rows had reserved signs on the seats. The Head, Mr Murphy, and his guests took up the centre seats, with other notables spreading out and back. When you peered out at them, it was like a sea with dark waters in the front (all suits, ties, long dresses, and wavy hair-dos) and bluey-green waves of sweaters and jeans at the back.

Although the rule for schoolkids was strictly approved school wear, no one paid attention. After three thirty time belonged to us, not the school. It gave students a chance to show off the latest gear and transform themselves from teenies into grown-up ravers and wannabes.

We classical performers, however, had no choice. Ours was far from casual wear. Bow ties and dark suits for the grown-ups, smart school uniform for the three wonder kids.

Our opening performance gained polite, if lukewarm applause, mainly from the front two rows. Our piece played while stragglers were still scraping chairs, locating seats in the dark. Fidgety Fee surprised us by playing so boldly and faultlessly that I half expected old 'Upstairs' to give her the solo spot. But my name was on the printed programme: 'Tom Goodall. Cello. "Yesterday" by Lennon/ McCartney'.

I was too nervous to watch the Spice Girl look-alikes, the rap singers, and the steel band that followed. Judging from the clapping, whoops, and whistles, they were all big hits.

Finally, to round off the evening, we trooped back on after the steel band. I could hear from the clatter in the hall that some were taking the opportunity to escape before the rush. As I passed my friend and centre-back Bobby, he whispered, 'Good luck, Tom. See if you can wake up the old geezer at the end of the row.'

I could see what he meant. As we took our seats on stage, I glanced towards this white-haired man with his eyes shut and mouth wide open. The funny sight gave me the giggles and helped me forget my nerves. A few rows back were Mum and Terry Wimbush. Mum was wearing her black concert outfit, Mr Wimbush was in dark jacket and red scarf. It was too dark to see their faces.

Just as Mr Stares dropped his hand to start our Tchaikovsky 'Andante Cantabile', a baby at the back let out a wail, setting off another infant and a spate of giggles from some kids. We ploughed on through the racket, trying to drown it out. But the baby duet won in the end.

My turn. No introduction. Just a shifting of chairs and music stands.

A cold sweat came over me. I needed the toilet badly.

Squeezing the cello hard to stop my knees knocking and barely able to hold my bow straight, I remembered the shy young woman at the Guildhall and how she'd been wrapped up in her music. And at the last moment Terry's words flashed through my brain: 'Focus on a face.'

I squinted round. There was the Head looking suitably calm and proud. Not him. The old snoozer. No. Mum was too far back. No one in the front row appealed to me. Then, standing next to the exit beside Snoozer was a bald, middle-aged man in a red sweater; he was holding one of the squawking babies.

He smiled apologetically from me to the baby as he rocked it back to sleep.

'You'll do,' I said to myself. 'You're old enough to be a Beatles fan.'

And I started playing (the word *pianissimo* ringing in my head).

It's weird hearing yourself for the first time, sitting all alone and faced by a sea of faces. The echoes come back at you off the walls. You hear the slightest rustle and stifled cough. Most of all, it's the silence. Even the babies were kind to me. Perhaps my lullaby had lulled them off. Some hope!

I knew the piece off by heart so I didn't really need to follow the music. Every so often I looked to the baby holder. He was smiling up at me, singing the words noiselessly to me, nodding his bald head.

I was coming to the end. Mr Wimbush's word drummed in my brain and flowed all the way down to my bow hand: *crescendo*. For the finale.

There, I'd got through it.

Silence. Not even a lukewarm clap. Nothing. Just a whispered 'Well done, Tom' from Fiona behind me.

Then someone started applauding. I'm sure it was Mum. The patter of raindrops steadily turned to hailstones.

The man in the red sweater must have dumped the baby into someone's arms; he had come up to the foot of the stage, his big hands slapping together and . . . tears rolling down his cheeks.

I could hear a familiar voice, 'Bravo! Bravo! Bravissimo!'

Someone in the front row shouted 'Encore! Encore!' and a voice from the back bawled out 'More!'

I didn't know any more! Apart from 'Haydn Was a Happy Man', but that wouldn't do here.

The Head saved the day. He was supposed to award the music prize for best performance. And as the lights went up, he climbed stiffly up the steps to the stage.

After thanking everyone for coming and everyone for playing, he announced, 'It is my pleasant duty to award this year's music prize to . . . Tom Goodall.'

Well, you could have knocked me down with a feather. I went as red as Mr Wimbush's silk scarf. Even my string colleagues were taken aback. After all, we were only the supporting act, like bookends to prop up the main performers. While Mr Stares was slapping me on the back, I was brought down to earth by the Head's next words.

'I'm sure I speak on behalf of everyone when I say: "Tom, one more time, please." '

More stormy applause.

This time the lights stayed on and I played for Mum.

'Thanks, Mum, for the cello, for delivering my papers, for being my best friend.'

'Jello'

My celebrity status was a mixed blessing. To most kids the music prize—a little silver cup—was the Devil's curse. If winning meant anything to them it was the *outside* recognition it brought—a recording contract, invitation for audition, photo in *The News*.

Hardly reward for a cello solo.

Any *school* award was worthless. Worse than that. It meant crossing the divide from Us to Them. From now on 'Goodall' was a name to be noted in the bully book—for future reference.

I had come out into the open. If you had to do something poncy, like dressing up as a girl, playing chess or classical music, you did so behind closed doors and drawn curtains, with as little fuss as possible. But to show off on stage, in school, before a few hundred people, was breaking the rules.

I had a taste of what was to come on the Monday. At break one of our rap stars came up to me with his bodyguards.

'You didn't win nuffink,' were his opening words.

I shrugged. There was no point in encouraging him. You never knew what he might be on: some kids came to school well stoned.

'Marko should've won,' a bodyguard snarled.

'I didn't pick the winner,' I said defensively.

'What d'ya expect, shithead?' Marko said, putting his pimply face into mine. 'They ain't gonna pick me if they can avoid it. And *you*, scumbag, gave 'em their chance.'

''S nuffink to do wiv moosik,' one of his mates added.

'It's about face, innit! So's Spud Murphy can show off: "See what *our* kids can do—play the jello".'

'Cello,' I corrected him without thinking.

The smack round the ear helped me think.

'Watchit, smart-arse. Or I'll stick your rotten jello up your arse. Lug that piece of shit to school again . . . '

Marko acted out shoving it up my backside before ambling off with his thugs.

So that was that. The string orchestra would have to make do without their celebrated cello. It was all right for violins: you could disguise them in a PE bag or tommy-gun case. But cello—that was a dead give-away.

I had to explain the situation to Mr Stares. He knew the score. He was upset, but understanding; he even suggested a quiet word in Marko's ear. Some hope. He knew as well as I did that it would only cause more grief. If there was anything worse than playing cello, it was dobbing to teachers.

You had to fight your own battles. No matter what teachers said, you were on your own against the bullies.

I can't say I was that bothered. Marko and his music-lovers weren't against me playing the cello. I just couldn't play it on school premises. There was still home and Mr Wimbush's.

The Warning went round school like wildfire. Even my football mates didn't mention how chuffed they were to have a cellist in goal. And if some unsuspecting teacher babbled on about how proud the class should be of the school's prizewinner, heads suddenly bowed over desks. No ears were redder, no head was lower than mine.

When I got home from school, Mum greeted me with a proud grin.

'Well, Major Tom, I bet your schoolfriends look up to you now.'

How wrong could she be.

42

'They'll *look me up* more likely!' I said.

She could tell something had happened. And when I told her the story, she sat down with a bump, lost for words.

'Not to worry,' I said to cheer her up. 'Mr Wimbush says all great musicians have a cross to bear. Mozart was beaten by his dad. Chopin was painfully shy. Boy George got laughed at.'

Mum smiled.

'I wouldn't class Boy George with Mozart and Chopin,' she murmured. 'Oh dear, Tom, what are we going to do?'

For the first time Mum was looking to me, the man of the house, for answers.

'Nothing!' I said firmly. 'I've explained to Mr Stares: I'm resigning from the Music Club. But I'm *not* giving up the cello and I *won't* desert Mr Wimbush. The bullies won't win, I'll practise twice as hard, just to spite them.'

'That's my boy,' said Mum.

Mr Wimbush was disappointed, but not that surprised.

'These things are sent to try us, Tom,' he said. 'Prejudice is a nasty thing. It's based on fear and ignorance. Fear of the unknown. Ignorance of why things happen the way they do. People aren't born prejudiced; society moulds them. As for good music, as long as the papers and TV feed punters on a diet of pre-digested pap—soaps, cartoons, pop music, and games shows—it's hard for people to get to know good music. It's like beautiful flowers trying to grow in a garden overrun with weeds.'

'I'm *not* giving up!'

He was surprised by my stubborn cry.

'The choice is yours, Tom,' he said quietly. 'As long as you want to play, I'll be here to help you.'

He smiled and mumbled to himself, 'Besides cakes and ale, people *need* jello music.'

43

Fans

Despite the bully ban on my cello, not all kids went along with it. No one actually marched up to Marko and punched him on the nose. My music didn't merit suicide. In any case, brute force wasn't the answer. Mr Wimbush was right: fear and prejudice had to be educated out of people.

In the days to come, when I might have basked in glory (instead of cringing in the shadows), a few hurried whispers helped cheer me up. Fidgety Fee and her fellow-violinist chose me as their 'special friend'—much to my embarrassment.

'We'll stand by you, Tom,' Fiona assured me. 'We think you rock.'

That did wonders for my reputation, reinforcing the 'nancy' tag Marko had stuck on me. But still, it *was* a kind gesture.

'My dad reckons you're fab,' added Fee's friend Eleanor. 'He was a Beatles fan when he was young. He even called me after one of their songs: "Eleanor Rigby".'

I wondered to myself whether he was the smiling baldy with the baby. It turned out he was.

'Dad says he's never heard a cello by itself before. You "pulled at his heartstrings" he said. Now he's saving up to buy one for my sister Michelle—she's only nine months.'

We all laughed at that. But inside I felt happy; my music had actually reached someone, maybe changed how they felt.

A few other kids went out of their way to congratulate

me. One was an Asian boy I'd never spoken to before. I'd noticed him once or twice, a bit of a loner. But since he was in the year above, I'd no cause for contact.

One lunchtime he came and sat next to me in the canteen. These days company was distinctly scarce—for fear of Marko and his friends putting the evil eye on camp followers.

'Hiya,' he said. 'Wanna crisp?'

'No, thanks,' I replied.

His sad brown eyes narrowed.

'Oh, go on, then,' I said with a change of heart. 'Thanks.'

'I'm Sanjeev,' he said between crisp munching.

'I'm Tom,' I responded politely, not wanting him to think I was prejudiced.

'Tom Goodall,' he said in admiring tones. 'You were really cool.'

'Yeah, well, you know,' I said uncertainly. 'Not everyone thinks so.'

'Pay no attention,' he said firmly. 'I'll be your friend if you like.'

That's all I needed. Two girl violinists and an Asian kid against the Marko gang. But there was another thing that warned me off the unwanted attentions of this Sanjeev. It wasn't colour. As long as he didn't mind my colour, I didn't mind his. No, it was something else, hard to put into words.

He reminded me a bit of David. Not in size: Sanjeev was as fit and slim as a gymnast. I suppose it was his Asian manner: delicate hand movements, the way he moved his head, his softly-spoken words, using proper grammar.

He was looking at me expectantly. All at once I realized he wanted an answer to his offer of friendship.

'Fine,' I said. 'Thanks a lot. See you around.'

With that I packed my empty lunchbox into my 'Portsmouth FC' bag and, biting on a green apple, I headed off for the loo. He followed. Now, sharing crisps was one thing. Having a wee together was quite another. People might start talking . . .

So I turned back and repeated firmly, 'See you around!'

He hesitated, then said quietly, 'I'd like to hear you again.'

'OK,' I said slowly. 'I'll think about it, all right?'

With that I turned my back and hurried off.

Although he didn't follow me into the lav, he was back at my side in the canteen next day. This time he offered me some Indian sweets. They were sweet and sticky. But there was a price to pay.

'When can I see you play?'

At first I thought he was talking about football. Then I recalled his strange request of the day before.

'Well, you can't really,' I muttered, mouth full of syrupy chews. 'I either go to lessons or I practise in my room.'

He thought over the options before choosing.

'I can come round if you like, after tea . . . As long as your mum and dad don't mind—you know what I mean.'

I was trapped. If I said no, that would involve Mum. I'm sure *she* wouldn't mind at all. And he might be thinking I was racist. There were plenty who were, in and outside school.

On the other hand, if I said yes, I'd have him interfering with my practice. Perhaps he sensed that.

'If you're worried about me putting you off, I'd be as quiet as a mouse, honest.'

I was beginning to realize how pop stars felt, fending off their fans. Sanjeev was apparently the first member of the 'Tom Goodall Fan Club'. No screaming and shouting. Just silent adoration.

I was running out of excuses.

'You'd be bored stiff,' I said as my final weak rebuff.

'Oh no. I'd *love* to listen.'

There's no accounting for taste!

'Go on then,' I conceded. 'Come round about six. I'll have finished tea and my paper round by then.'

'I'll give you a hand with your papers,' he said, eyes shining. 'Then you'll have more time to practise.'

What was I letting myself in for? The price of fame . . . My resistance was shot to pieces.

'Please yourself,' I muttered. 'I'll be at JG's at four thirty, when the papers come out.'

That's how it all began. Something beyond my control.

Paper Chase

I didn't normally have friends round. Come to think of it, I didn't normally have friends. End of story. True, I had my football mates, and the occasional scatterbrain who dropped in to check on homework or football venues. I didn't care about them branding me a mummy's boy.

So when I got in and told Mum about Sanjeev, she had a shock.

'Oh Tom, why didn't you warn me? Just look at the mess. What *will* your friend think?'

I tried to tell her he wasn't really my friend, just someone from school who'd stuck to me. But she was too preoccupied: bustling round the living room with duster and hoover, plumping up the settee cushions, straightening the pictures.

Then she dashed out to the convenience store for jam doughnuts—something that was never part of our low fat diet.

When I reached JG's on my mountain bike, there was No. 1 Fan waiting outside. He was sitting sideways on his bike, grinning awkwardly.

'Hold on while I see if the papers are in,' I said. 'I won't be a tick.'

Mr Gant was as grumpy as ever. He was one of those sad-faced people who can't open his mouth without moaning.

'Is he with *you*?' he asked, stabbing a brown-stained finger at the window.

I nodded.

'Well, for pity's sake keep him outside. I don't want his sort in here nicking my stock.'

'Why should he do that, Mr Gant?' I asked, acting all innocent-like.

'Never you mind,' he muttered, not rising to the bait. 'Just get those papers out.'

He'd already counted out the evening edition and left the address list on top of the freshly-smelling print. Although I knew the deliveries by heart, there were always one or two struck off for not paying their bill.

Stuffing the stack of *The News* into my fluorescent bag, I slung it over my shoulder and re-joined Sanjeev.

'Let me carry the bag,' he begged. 'Please.'

I was beginning to enjoy fame.

'Please yourself,' I said, unhitching the heavy bag and transferring it to him. Through the window I could see a cross face glowering at us; two fingers were drumming on a wristwatch—to warn about wasting time. Once down the road I gave a two-fingered salute of my own before stopping by a block of maisonettes.

'You stay put and keep an eye on the bikes,' I ordered. 'Don't let them out of your sight. They'd pinch the hair off your head round this way.'

When I'd finished running up and down stairwells, pushing papers through letterboxes, and irritating Alsatian man-eaters on the inside, I returned to Sanjeev. Just in the nick of time.

He was surrounded by a band of teenage thugs. One was poking him in the chest and taunting him.

'G'is a read o' yer paper, Paki! Or I'll report ya as an illegal imm'grant.'

Sanjeev was trying to explain.

'I'm not from Pakistan, I'm Indian. And I am not an illegal immigrant. I was born here; so was my family. We have a shop on Allaway Avenue.'

They loved that, mimicking his accent and poking him all the harder. Before they could cause more trouble, they saw me approaching. Not that my appearance had them quaking in their boots. But I provided a second Aunt Sally for their taunts.

'What d'ya know? If it ain't our little nancy boy,' cried the spikey-haired leader. 'Our musical paper boy.'

I recognized him: the elder brother of one of the Marko gang. Like many older boys on the estate, he'd left school and been out of work ever since. He had nothing to do all day save watch telly and roam the streets looking for trouble. 'Darkies' and 'nancies' were both fair game in his book, giving colour to his otherwise drab existence. To his mind, 'darkies' were taking jobs he should have filled.

If it hadn't been for some bare-chested guy, leaning over a balcony above us, the mood might have turned really nasty.

'Hey, you!' he bawled. 'Get up 'ere. Yer soddin' mobile's been ringin' for ages!'

That was our chance.

Grabbing the bag from Sanjeev, I pedalled off round the corner, with him hot on my tail. I'd leave that block's deliveries till last.

'Phew,' I panted as we reached safety. 'Now I know how zebras feel being hunted by a pack of hungry lions. I don't normally get any grief on this round. The odd cat-call, nothing more.'

'Sorry, it's all my fault,' he said upset. 'I didn't mean to cause trouble.'

'It's *not* your fault,' I said. 'It's those yobboes. Ignorant morons!'

'It *is* my fault,' he insisted. 'I get it all the time. So do my parents and sisters. The shop has had its windows broken three times this year.'

I looked at him and felt guilty. How selfish of me. I hadn't even bothered to ask anything about him: where he lived, what his family did, what he got up to in his spare time . . .

'So you're on Allaway Avenue, are you?' I said in between slipping papers into letterboxes.

'We live above the shop—Malik's.'

Allaway was off my beaten track; we had our own shopping parade round the corner. But I knew where he meant. Slap bang in the middle of 'Nowhereland', as it was known because of derelict buildings and vandalism. Not long back—'within living memory', as Mum put it, which meant four or five years ago—we had big firms just down the road: Smith's Crisps, Johnson & Johnson Baby Products, Twilfit Corsets.

Now all packed up and gone.

Money was tight. The old ones were scared. The young ones were angry. No jobs. No prospects. No dosh. They got their kicks from wacky baccy, booze, and popping pills, paid for by raiding homes and shops.

It was a brave—or Asian—shopkeeper who stuck it out on Allaway. Even the fish 'n' chip shop was Chinese.

'Come on, Sanjeev,' I said wearily. 'Let's get home.'

The News

Not only was Mum getting tea and doughnuts ready, the table was laid with a fresh tablecloth. And she was having a good old chinwag with a visitor. Terry Wimbush. They both made a fuss of my new friend, telling him all they knew about India—which didn't take long. Mr Wimbush boasted of preparing a 'mean curry' himself.

'Mind you, I'm not a patch on you Indians,' he said modestly. 'I can never get the chapattis right, you know, light and fluffy, as they do at the Gandhi and Bombay House.'

'Actually, we never go to restaurants,' said Sanjeev. 'My mother and sisters do all the cooking.'

'But I guess you all meet up, at church and that,' said Mr Wimbush.

'Not really,' said Sanjeev patiently. 'You see, the restaurants are run by people from Bangladesh; they're Muslims. So they attend the mosque in Southsea. We go to the Hindu temple.'

That squashed poor Mr Wimbush. For once he was lost for words.

'I say, haven't I put my big feet in it,' he exclaimed, throwing up his hands. 'You see, Jeanette, it doesn't do to be too clever.'

Mum agreed. She didn't know much about India either.

'What I *do* know,' she sang out from the kitchen, 'is that even if the doughnuts come from down the road, the tea is Indian.'

Sanjeev said she made a really delicious cup of tea. That pleased Mum no end.

'I hear you were at the school concert,' she said to Sanjeev as she brought in the hot doughnuts.

'Tom was wonderful,' he said, looking at me all doe-eyed.

'*If* I'm any good,' I said, 'I owe it to Mr Wimbush. It's his cello and his fantastic teaching.'

'*Was* my cello,' said Terry Wimbush. 'Once you give someone a present, it's *theirs* to keep. You've made us all proud with *your* cello.'

Sanjeev was looking puzzled.

'What I don't understand,' he said to no one in particular, 'is why playing the cello makes Tom a nancy boy. What is a "nancy"?'

If he'd dropped his hot tea over Mum's lap, she wouldn't have jumped more. Mr Wimbush shifted uneasily on the settee. I burst out laughing.

'Where did you get that?' Mum asked, as if she hadn't heard properly.

'Oh, some boys at school, and again on the paper round.'

'I see,' she said.

She was always saying 'I see-ee-ee' when she was stuck for words. This time she looked hopefully to Mr Wimbush.

He cleared his throat, like a vicar in the pulpit.

'A nancy,' he began. 'A nancy, let's see. First, it's short—or long—for the girl's name, Ann. *Nod a lodda people know dat!*'

He said the last sentence in a cockney accent. It broke the tension, and we all laughed too loudly.

'Second, it's a word about anyone who's effeminate; a man who acts a bit womany. Usually, a gay man, a homosexual. They get called all sorts of silly names—"nancy" is about the mildest. And third, with some people, playing or even liking classical music is regarded as girly, stuff for cissies. It's not, of course. Almost all the great composers, conductors, musicians are men. Take your pick.'

Sanjeev obviously didn't share the English reserve. He came straight out with things. Perhaps he didn't dare ask such questions at home.

'I get called lots of names,' he said matter-of-factly. 'Paki, wog, darky . . . At school I too get called "nancy boy". Yet I don't play music at all.'

Both Mum and Mr Wimbush were clearly embarrassed. Neither knew what to say. Finally, Mum coughed and said, 'Pay no attention. It's because you're different, that's all.'

'Do you ever get called names, Mr Wimbush?' Sanjeev suddenly asked.

That put him—and Mum—on the spot. Naturally, Mum had told me his secret. But it wasn't for general telling. I could see he didn't know what to say. He could hardly come out with it: 'I'm homosexual, you know. I get called nancy too!'

Mum came to his rescue.

'I call Mr Wimbush plenty of names,' she said. 'He's my sweety pie, my darling man, my honey pot. But if he's naughty, I call him a "wicked old devil". Now then, Sanjeev, if you don't mind, Mr Wimbush and I want to watch the six o'clock news. I know Tom's promised to play for you upstairs.'

She turned to me with a glassy-eyed stare.

'Tom, take Sanjeev up to your room, there's a good boy.'

Mum got up and switched on the telly.

Meanwhile, Sanjeev and I finished off our tea in silence, with half an eye on the flickering screen. It showed a photo of a sweet little girl in school uniform; such a cheeky dimpled smile on her face. The newsreader was saying how she'd disappeared from her home and police were searching for her.

'How terrible,' said Mum. 'Poor little mite. That's only a few miles down the road. What on earth could have happened to her?'

'Oh, she'll turn up. They always do,' said Terry comfortingly.

'But what if she doesn't?' said Mum with a worried frown.

'Well, Jeanette, that's no concern of ours,' he retorted sadly.

How could he know that it was soon to become his concern? *All* our concerns. Big time!

The Letter

Big event. A letter came for me. 'Mr T. Goodall'.

 The top left hand corner of the long white envelope bore the city Star and Crescent crest. Mum was sure it was tax. I reckoned football. We were both wrong. It wasn't my first tax demand on paper round earnings, or a call to help Pompey out of their goalkeeping crisis.

Dear Mr Goodall,

 It gives me pleasure to invite you to audition for the County Youth Orchestra. Auditions for violin/ viola/cello/double bass will be held (Saturday 5 August at 11 a.m.) at the Great Hall, Winchester.

 Indicate availability below and return in the enclosed pre-paid envelope.

 No alternative date can be arranged.

 Auditions will consist of Theory and Practical (a short prepared piece of your choice, and a set of unseen exercises).

 Yours,

 G. K. Fry

YES/NO

 Charming. What if we were holidaying in the South Seas? What if I was struck down with rabies? What if I had a football match? My entire music career could be up the spout.

 Mum was unsympathetic.

'We can afford only Southsea, not the South Seas. You don't catch rabies in Britain. There's no school football in the summer holidays.'

'But, Mum . . .'

To tell the truth, I was scared stiff. Playing my cello in front of Mum and Mr Wimbush, even school, was fair enough—though look where school had got me! But playing with all those arty-farty types wasn't my scene.

That cut no ice with Mum. She was positively glowing and already planning what I was to wear . . .

'Oh Tom, when I was a girl I dreamed of playing in the Youth Orchestra at county level. They go all over the world, you know—to the Isle of Wight, Jersey, Holland.'

If there was a 'Mum expression' I hated most it was 'When I was a girl', as if the world hadn't moved on in twenty-five years. Anyway, the Isle of Wight wasn't that exotic; I'd played football there.

'It's only an audition,' I said, half agreeing. 'I'll probably make a mess of it even if I do go.'

'*No you won't!*' she cried. 'Mr Wimbush and I will see to that!'

Why did I have this feeling that the pair of them were living their lives through me? They were going to make me succeed where they had failed. Like those dads who lined the touchline of a Saturday morning, bawling and swearing:

'Get stuck in!'

'Clobber the bastard!'

'You bloody useless tart!'

I knew I wasn't being fair. Mum had never had a real chance: 'She could have been a professional.' So Mr Wimbush had said. As for Terry Wimbush, he'd suffered from gammy fingers. Still, August was over five months away. The earth could be zapped by aliens before then or taken over by music-hating zombies.

Right away Mum gave Terry a bell. I'd certainly made her happy. She was fairly chirping away on the phone as if she'd won the lottery.

When I went round to Mr Wimbush that evening, we made plans. Or, rather, he made plans for me.

'Number One,' he said, 'scales practice. They're bound to pick a scale with lots of sharps and flats, as well as a hard exercise to play by sight. Number Two, a short piece, eh?'

'How about ''Yesterday''?' I said hopefully.

He shook his head.

'Horses for courses, old son. The Beatles might not go down too well with those Starchy Archies. In any case, how do they *know* about you? Have you thought of that?'

I hadn't. Now it suddenly dawned on me.

'Someone heard ''Yesterday'' at the school concert.'

'Yep. So we'll surprise them. Something old, something new. What do *you* think?'

'Elgar's Cello Concerto,' I suggested. 'That's nice.'

He rocked back in his chair, giving one of his horse whinnies, his ruddy face creased in smiles.

'One day, Tommy. Don't run before you can walk. Keep it simple. I'll ask Jeanette's advice. She has an ear for catchy tunes.'

Between them they came up with 'Ave Maria'. It apparently reminded Mum of the 'Hail Mary' prayer she used to say as a girl in the cathedral.

By my next lesson, Terry Wimbush had the music all ready: four stiff pages covered in squiggles. He hummed it through, singing the first two words: 'Ave Maria'. That was all he knew.

'Lots of composers have put that prayer to music,' he explained. 'This one is by a young Austrian called Franz Schubert. He was the son of a poor schoolmaster, intensely shy, never married, died at 31.'

Are all musicians weird or what? They're a bit like shooting stars—zoom across the sky in a blaze of light, then—phut!—fizzle out. Mozart, Chopin, Schubert. Shame.

Still, I don't think young Franz would have taken to me murdering his lovely song. The simplest tunes are the hardest to play.

The Second Letter

No sooner had I received my first-ever letter than a second arrived. Not at the house. I found it in my school locker. Someone had slipped it between the cracks at the bottom. It must have been a tight squeeze because the envelope was all squashed up like a concertina.

No one had sent me letters before. Well, I didn't count the scribbled Valentine with red love hearts all over it. Valentine cards are supposed to be secret, no names, just love messages. But not only did this scrap of paper bear two initials—'F' and 'E'—it was delivered personally by my fiddling friends.

They went to great lengths to declare their undying love, writing S W A L K on the envelope and drawing a music stave in yellow at the bottom, with pink notes on it. Clever, huh? When I hummed the notes to myself I couldn't help smiling. Sweet. 'I just called to say I love you . . . '

Valentines weren't my cup of tea. I'd *never-ever* sent one. Never fancied anyone enough to declare my love, even as a joke. But you always had kids boast about how many cards they'd received. Needless to say, Marko claimed ten. He'd probably sent them all himself.

Back to this crumpled letter. I'd stuffed it in my jacket pocket quickly, just in case some joker jumped out, shouting, 'Wanker!' Who knows? It could be a death threat!

So it wasn't till I was safe in my bedroom that I fished the letter out. Mum was 'busy' downstairs watching telly; I'd done my paper round and wolfed down our fish 'n' chip tea—we always had fish on Fridays. I'd cleaned my football boots ready for the match tomorrow—if the pitches were playable. You only had to spit on our playing fields for the groundsmen to declare them flooded. ALL MATCHES OFF FOR THE WEEKEND! Lazy gits!

I smoothed out the envelope and slid my thumbnail along the top. Someone had well and truly gummed it down. If I was expecting a long chatty letter or a three-word death threat: 'YOU WILL DIE!' I was in for disappointment and relief.

It was a note in pencil, good English, just one side of unlined paper smelling of flowers. The signature was over the page. I looked there first, but couldn't make it out. If anything, it resembled a spider tripping over its own feet.

Whoever wrote it at least got my name right: 'Dear Tom . . .'

I read on. The more I read the more astonished, shocked, frightened I became. It was like biting into some unknown fruit—kiwi or passion—not knowing what to expect, yet finding several tastes all at once. Bitter *and* sweet.

Dear Tom,

Please forgive me writing to you. It's just that I can write down what I can't say.

Please, please, don't tell anyone, and tear up the letter as soon as you read it.

I wish I could really, really understand how I feel. It's so hard. No one understands me.

*What I know is that **I love you**.*

That's all. Don't be angry.

I don't expect you to love me back. I'm a boy, you see.

Love you,

(clumsy spider . . .)

My hands were damp and trembling. I read the letter through a few times, trying to make it out. My first thought was that it was a put-on, someone taking the mick. Tom Goodall was always good for a laugh. The 'jello kid', the 'nancy boy', the 'prize prick'.

The trouble was the longer I lay on my bed thinking about it, the more excited I got. Most of all, the keener I was to discover *who* my unknown admirer was. Was he kind, sensitive, handsome? Or ugly, smelly, pimply?

I picked up the envelope for a clue, sniffing it, feeling the edges, examining the writing. What would Sherlock Holmes deduce from it? There *was* something. A slight spicy whiff. Old Spice after-shave? Maybe. Not that it rang any bells.

'Tom!' came a shout. 'Practice time.'

I didn't really need reminding. Practice was a bind, sometimes very boring, depending on my mood, though it did turn my mind off my worries. Yet somehow the 'love letter' had put a spring in my step—or its musical equivalent: buzz to my bow, gloss on my glissando, chuff to my cello . . .

I tiptoed up and down the scales, sailed through the exercises and, for the first time, caressed the most moving music from 'Ave Maria'. If my cello could sing, it would have sung the most beautiful love song: 'To My Unknown Admirer!'

Castration

I said nothing to Mum about some boy fancying me. When I'd finished my practice and homework, I skipped down the stairs two at a time—much to Mum's annoyance.

'Don't run. Walk. You'll end up breaking your neck one of these days!'

I buttered her up with a kiss on the top of her head.

'Shush,' she said. 'I want to hear this.'

We sat together, watching the Nine O'Clock News.

'The body of a young girl has been found,' the man was saying in a hushed voice. 'Police fear it may be that of the missing schoolgirl.'

On to the screen came a policeman in civvies, sitting at a table bristling with microphone bayonets pointing at his chest. He was talking in a slow, clear voice as if reading out the football results.

'This morning police found the body of a young girl in a field. She had been strangled. Items of clothing were discovered near the body. If anyone has information, anything at all, about a person or persons acting suspiciously in the area, or about any vehicle seen parked in the neighbourhood, will they contact the police on the following number . . . '

I'd rarely seen Mum so upset and angry. It was as if she took it personally.

'Who'd want . . . to do a thing . . . like that,' she said, choking on her words. 'To a poor, innocent little girl!'

She caught her breath before spitting out, 'Men like that need castrating!'

That's the second time I'd come across the word. The first was in a music book; it referred to singers called *castrati*—men who'd had their nuts cut off in boyhood, so as to keep their voices high—a bit like mine despite all I did to add some *basso profundo*! I guessed what Mum meant, but I asked her all the same.

'What's "castrating", Mum?'

'Cut their things off,' she said crossly. 'So's they can't go round molesting little children!'

I didn't ask her what 'molesting' meant because I suddenly realized something. And I understood why Mum was getting her knickers in a twist. So the little girl hadn't simply been murdered . . .

She switched off the telly and sat staring into space. When Mum got really mad, her face and neck went almost as red as her hair. Like now. To calm her down I dredged up Mr Wimbush's words.

'That's no concern of ours, Mum, is it? We can't do anything about it.'

Her mind was so far away that I thought she hadn't heard me. But she evidently had, for after a bit she said quietly, like a cat about to pounce on a mouse:

'Oh, yes, there is! There's *got* to be! It goes on all the time.'

'What does, Mum?'

I hadn't heard about many girls being strangled.

'Child abuse,' she said abruptly. 'Dirty old men who can't keep their filthy hands off kids. Perverts. Paedophiles.'

She turned on me.

'If anyone tries anything dirty with you, Tom, you'd tell me, wouldn't you?'

''Course, Mum. I don't reckon we've got any paedo— whatever their face is—on our estate.'

She continued staring into space, seeing dirty old men

on the opposite wall, just below the picture of five cows grazing peacefully in a meadow.

'We have, Tom. Oh, yes, we have. They don't hang a sign on their door, saying "I'M A PERVERT". We probably have more per square mile than anywhere in the city.'

She could see from my frown I didn't know what she was on about.

'You see, when the Council has to rehouse "problem people"—perverts, say, fresh out of prison—they have to put them somewhere. Somewhere cheap and big enough to swallow them up, where they won't be noticed. Do you see?'

I did see. Although I didn't dare tell her, I immediately remembered some bloke on my paper round; he was always trying to get me indoors on one excuse or another. I knew a boy at school who told me what went on behind the door.

'Easy money,' he said. 'Five quid for a hand job.'

I knew such things went on. Most kids did. But we didn't think they were dangerous. The little girl's murder put a different complexion on it.

'We ought to know exactly *who* they are,' Mum was saying, as if making up her mind.

'You said they don't hang out signs,' I reminded her.

'No, but *someone* must know, someone at the Council.'

Once Mum got her teeth into something, she didn't let go. There and then she wrote two letters: one to the Council and one to *The News*.

'Carrot and stick for the donkey,' she said. 'If the Council doesn't take my carrot, they'll get plenty of stick from the paper. And it won't be a pretty sight: *"Why our politicians put perverts in our midst! We demand to know who they are!"* '

She stuck on two blue stamps and dashed out to post

her letters. 'Strike while the iron's hot!' she flung back as she flew through the door.

I knew what she meant. Mum blew all hot and cold. One moment full of passion to act, the next wondering why she'd bothered.

After several days she still had no response from the Council. But two days later someone phoned her up from the 'Woman's Section' of the local paper. The reporter wanted to know Mum's views on paedophiles, her age, her husband's job, how many children she had, that sort of 'personal touch'. And, by the way, 'Was it all right to send round a photographer—to get a shot of her and her little boy?'

'I don't see how age comes into it,' grumbled Mum, never one to volunteer her personal details. 'Nor what it's got to do with anyone whether I'm married or not!'

I think she was beginning to wish she hadn't started this.

So this guy comes round in a van with THE NEWS printed in big letters on the sides. He carried this heavy camera. After dozens of shots of Mum and me, he said cheerio and that was that. We heard nothing more until the following Thursday.

When I got to JG's for my paper round, Mr Gant had a rare hint of a smile beneath his sweaty bald head.

'I see your mother's in the news,' he grunted. 'Quite right too! Hanging's too good for 'em!'

For a moment I didn't know what he was talking about. Then the penny dropped. I grabbed my bag of newspapers and rushed off. Luckily, my Fan Club member had Scouts every Thursday, so I was left on my own. Once round the corner, I stopped, whipped out a paper and glanced at the headline:

LOCAL WOMAN DEMANDS ACTION
ON PAEDOPHILES

The top of the paper carried a picture of Mum and me, and a note: 'See Woman's Section, p. 27.'

Quickly turning to the pull-out section, I took one look at the first page . . . and nearly puked. It had a half-page picture of Mum giving me a cuddle, under which was the 'story': 'Thirty-three-year-old Jeanette Goodall, a single mother and housewife of 46 High Lawn Way, calls on the Council for action. The fiery redhead would willingly castrate perverts living in ''safe houses''. She demands the right to know their addresses . . . '

More of the same spread over two pages.

If it weren't for fear of old Gant booting me out, I'd have dumped the bag and papers in a muddy ditch. Pulling my baseball cap down over my eyes, I sped round the neighbourhood, getting rid of the papers before anyone could recognize me.

What a way to get famous!

Sanjeev

Everyone, they say, has fifty seconds (or is it fifteen minutes?) of fame during their lifetime. For the second time in six months I became a celebrity. But this time I'd *really* made it: my picture was in *The News*! Even teachers I'd never met stopped to say 'Hi, Tom.' My mate Sanjeev brought me a whole box of Indian sweets with a note from his mum.

'Please thank your mother for speaking up. We are so glad our son has a good, decent friend.'

When I showed Mum, she shrugged.

'I seem to have stirred up a hornet's nest,' she muttered. 'Anyway, the sweets'll come in handy. We're having chicken curry tonight.'

'I could tell that halfway down the street,' I said.

'Mr Wimbush's coming round, bringing the chapattis—according to Sanjeev's recipe. So don't dawdle on your paper round.'

I rode off to the paper shop, curry smells clinging to the hairs of my nostrils. As I was cycling along, a far-off bell rang in my brain. Sniff-sniff. Curry. Sniff-sniff. Squashed letter. That was the link. It wasn't Old Spice after-shave, it was curry I'd smelt on the envelope!

'Elementary, dear Watson!' said my Sherlock Holmes, congratulating himself on his powers of deduction.

Sanjeev! It had to be. Why hadn't I thought of him before? Not that I'd thought of *anyone* except a joker, one of my mates trying to take the rise out of me. So the letter could be genuine, after all?

There he was, my secret admirer, sitting on his bike

saddle, looking out for me. These days he waited out of sight of the newsagent's—after Mr Gant had shooed him off. 'Bad for business!' he'd moaned.

Should I confront him? Best wait a bit. Now that it was serious, I'd have to give it careful consideration. A real love letter from a boy. Wow! Now what? We could hardly make a date, hold hands, and go out together.

'Hi, Sanjeev,' I called. 'My mum says ta for the sweets. They'll go with our curry tonight.'

He smiled shyly.

Since his brush with local youths, we did the round on foot together, with me keeping him in sight at all times. Mr Gant let us leave our bikes in his back shed; since the round now took half the time, he didn't complain. As always, Sanjeev carried the heavy bag, I did the deliveries.

It was a fine early summer evening and we were both sweating as we trotted back to the shop.

'Thanks, Sanjeev, you're a mate,' I said.

He'd got the bag strap tangled in his school jacket. Despite the warm evening, his mum always made him wear a jacket—'to look smart'.

'Here, let me help,' I said, unhitching it.

As I went to lift off the strap, our hands accidentally touched: white on brown, warm on cold. For the briefest of moments we stood looking at each other, scared and uncertain. I snatched my hand away as if stung by a bee. Yet at once I felt guilty as I saw the hurt in his sad eyes.

'Sorry,' I said.

I don't know what I was sorry about. But when we went to fetch our bikes, I said to him quietly, 'Sanjeev, I know you care. I got your note.'

I gave his arm a squeeze.

'It's all so confusing,' I said. 'I'd best do the papers alone for a bit, OK?'

In silence, he wheeled his bike around and cycled quickly off towards Allaway Avenue. I was glad it was out. But it didn't make me feel easier.

Halfway up our garden path I was aware of two senses: smell and hearing. Curry stew and the Wimbush whinny. Both cheered me up no end. For a start, I was starving hungry. And then there was Terry Wimbush . . .

No one who came into contact failed to like him. Whether it was his nature, or whether he played it up I don't know; but his every expression was that bit over the top. He was always laughing at his own jokes. Yet it was his giggling, not the joke, that had you in stitches.

But Terry Wimbush was more than a jester. No one knew more about music than him. No one had music pumping through his veins like him. He lived it, felt what others didn't, like an artist seeing beautiful pictures in a pool of lilies. And, like an artist, he had that inner eye, that sixth sense.

Whenever I met him I learned something new. This time was no different.

'Now then, Tommy, Peter Tchaikovsky. What can you tell me about him? They could ask you that at your audition.'

'He's Russian,' I said warily. 'He must be a bit cranky, otherwise he wouldn't be a great composer. His music? Ummm. "Andante Cantabile"—for string quartet. Ballets—*Swan Lake*, *Sleeping Beauty* . . . '

Mum couldn't wait to get in on the act. From the kitchen she bawled out, '*Nutcracker*, "None but the Lonely Heart" from *Eugene Onegin*.'

Terry clapped, shouting, 'Bravo! Bravo! Yes, yes. Music truly from the heart. Cranky? Of course. He used to get terribly down in the dumps, what they called "manic depression". But what made it worse he also had a guilty secret: "I am the Love that dare not speak its name", as

Oscar Wilde's friend Lord Alfred Douglas put it. So the white and black swans in *Swan Lake*, Odette and Odile, are really the two sides of his own nature.'

He could have gone on like that all night. But Mum put a stop to it.

'Come on, Terry, don't go filling Tom's head with all that stuff. He won't know what you're talking about.'

Oh, Mum! But I do. At least, I'm beginning to understand.

Note: must listen to more Tchaikovsky.

Gossip

And another thing about Terry Wimbush. He loved gossip. 'Oh, I say, did you know?', 'Well I never, who'd have thought it?', 'I shouldn't really be telling you this, but . . . '

So you'd cock an ear and learn of scandal from one end of the estate to the other. Neighbours knew Terry was harmless and a mine of rich gossip, so they stopped to exchange titbits in the street. It was through Terry that we came to hear of the mutterings 'on the Green'.

'Do you know,' he said, beckoning our heads closer and glancing round to see if the walls had wagging ears, 'some residents are taking action. They're so upset over that poor little girl's murder. Do you know, they still haven't found her killer. What a swine.'

He sat back, looking shocked at his own words, as if he'd just told us the sky had fallen on his head that morning. Then he leant forward, a fistful of chapatti in one hand, forkful of curry in the other.

'It's all thanks to you, Jeanette. They've taken a leaf out of your book. You're an example to all women. They look up to you.'

I could see Mum viewed her heroine role in a different light.

'A group of mothers did ask me to join them,' she admitted; 'be a sort of spokeswoman. But I'm not fussed. I've said my piece and that's that. I didn't like the way the press twisted my words for their own ends. That's out of order.'

'What ends, Mum?' I was genuinely puzzled.

'Sell more papers, of course!' she said crossly.

Now Terry Wimbush looked shocked. 'Oh, I say, you are an awful cynic,' he exclaimed. 'You had your say—and quite right too. It needed saying. And they printed your words.'

'Yes, but in the wrong order,' said Mum heatedly.

She was going red again. And it wasn't from the curry.

'Age and marital status, I ask you! They made me look like a bitter old man-hater. I *didn't* say I'd willingly castrate all perverts. They asked me if I thought castration was an option, and, as a joke, I said it's a pity you can't neuter some men like dogs. But they made it sound as if I was serious.'

'Pity,' said Terry gravely, his mind evidently on other things. 'They'd make such lovely singers.'

Mum exploded. 'Your trouble, Terry Wimbush, is that you reduce everything to music . . . '

I didn't have a chance to hear Terry's response because the phone rang.

'Oh darn, just when I had him on the spot!' said Mum, wiping her mouth and hands on a tissue and hurrying into the passage. We listened to her 'yes, no, yes, no' before switching attention back to the meal. The main reason for Mr Wimbush's visit was the approaching audition. He'd fitted in an extra weekly lesson at our place.

'Any more hassle at school?' he asked.

'Not really. With Mum's bit in the paper, my stock's gone up—for the moment.'

'No more ''nancy boy'' taunts?'

'Just the opposite: they see me as queer-basher champion. Just 'cos me and Mum have our mugs in the piece on perverts.'

'Ah, reflected glory, Tom. But beware: *sic transit gloria*

73

mundi, as the Romans used to say. ''Thus passes the glory of the world . . . '' It won't last.'

'Great!' I mumbled, putting out the fire in my mouth with a glass of water. 'If I had to choose, I'd rather be a ''ponce'' than a queer basher.'

At that moment, Mum rejoined us.

'Now, where was I? Oh yes, giving Terry a right bashing . . . '

We looked at each other and burst out laughing. Mum wasn't in on the joke.

'Who was that, Mum?' I asked.

'Most odd,' she said. 'Someone from a Sunday newspaper, didn't say which one. Sounded concerned. Said how delicate these matters were. I'd boldly shown a lead for others to follow, stirred the conscience of the nation . . . '

'Ooh, Jeanette,' cooed Terry Wimbush, 'you are a one, a national hero now.'

'I wouldn't go that far,' she said with a modest smile. 'One of their top reporters is coming down from London for an interview. It'll give me a chance to put the record straight.'

I didn't know what to think. The last thing I wanted was us being in the news again. If our mugs were plastered all over the Sundays, alongside Posh and Becks, Queenie and the princes, what would my mates say?

We finished the meal, had a cup of tea, and washed our hands. Mum's curry and Terry's chapattis were declared a great success—by Mum and Terry.

Now to work: C major scale, exercises, Franz's song.

Even if I did fail my audition, it certainly wouldn't be for want of trying. As Mum had said, she and Terry *wouldn't let me*!

On the Green

Events moved fast. A meeting was to be held on the Green, as we called the strip of 'grass' opposite the shopping parade. Normally it belonged to dogs like our Paddy and other bounding, burrowing bundles of mischief. They were the 'aristocrats' with homes to go to. But moth-eaten strays *lived* on the Green, used it as bed, board, and private convenience.

Being doggy property, the 'Green' wasn't actually green at all, but a scruffy, polka-dot mud grey, a barren desert free of bush, hedge, and flower bed. No crocus, daff, or daisy dared poke its head above the dog turds.

No one had used the Green as church hall since the Sally Army had held a jumble sale there. But the skies had opened up and tipped down rain and hail on them. They never did it again, regarding the Green, like the residents, as godforsaken.

Our Green was all that was left of once-virgin lower slopes, overlooking the port and dockyard. After the Stukas and doodlebugs had reduced most of the city to rubble, the postwar survivors had moved house to this green and pleasant land.

By the time I came into the world, it was no longer green and pleasant.

Out of curiosity, Mum took me down to the 'meeting'. No one seemed to be in charge; no one even knew who had called the meeting or put out the leaflets that had come through doors and appeared on shop windows.

Are you worried about your children? Do you know that convicted paedophiles live among you?

Act before it is too late!

Come to a meeting on the Green Friday 7.30.

RAP

Since the leaflet was signed RAP, I naturally assumed that my musical friends, Marko and his rappers, were behind it. But looking at the small print Mum read out 'Residents Against Paedophiles' at the bottom.

'Summat fishy here,' Mum had decided. 'Not many round here can spell "paedophiles", let alone say it. I reckon it's outsiders trying to stir up bother.'

What with that murdered girl hogging the news, feelings were running high. A big crowd had gathered. No one seemed to know what for exactly. Still, the evening was warm and nothing much was on telly. Some young girls were skipping and playing tag; boys were standing around poking fun at likely targets; men were chatting gravely; mums and grans were herding young kids about them, screeching and threatening.

Everyone was waiting for something to happen.

Round about eight o'clock, a hush suddenly came over the Green. A small, middle-aged man had climbed on to a soapbox. We'd never seen him before. He was nattily dressed, not like our lot, in a dark suit and white tie, black shirt and old-fashioned grey jumper. The smartness of his clothes was offset by his shaven head and heavy stubble. He reminded me of an ageing skinhead rock star.

'Attention, residents!' he cried in a high-pitched voice.

You could tell the moment he spoke he wasn't local. Not posh. More a mixture of vicar's drone and sergeant major's bark. He talked in short bursts, like machine-gun fire.

'You good people!' *Rat-tat-tat!* 'You care about your kids!' *Bang-bang-bang!* 'RAP was set up to help you!' *R-A-P, Rap-rap-rap!* 'Residents Against Paedophiles is your answer to official inactivity. We will hunt down all perverts, all child molesters, all the monsters in your midst. We demand to know where they live! Out the scum!'

He paused, chest puffed out, hands on hips, expecting a roar of approval.

A few uncertain claps and cheery shouts encouraged him to continue. But, it turned out, he wasn't about to hog the limelight.

'There are men and women among you who *know* the addresses of perverts. When these monsters are sent down for their vile crimes, the papers print their names and addresses, don't they? Libraries have back numbers of newspapers. So . . . ? Someone—a neighbour, relative, friend—*must* know something! You must have *heard* whispers, rumours, kids talking . . . '

He paused again, expecting streams of volunteers to rush forward.

A few men laughed nervously among themselves; women looked away in case his stare fixed on them; kids glanced at parents, as if to say: 'I don't know nuffin', honest!'

Just when it looked as if the meeting would fizzle out, a blonde woman of about Mum's age, with spiky hair and pale face, detached herself from a knot of women and children. She was helped on her way by a lumpy older woman, shoving her forward and shouting, 'Go on, gal, tell 'em!'

As the middle-aged skinhead stepped down from the box, his work done, the woman climbed up unsteadily, looking anxious and unsure of herself.

'I got five kids,' she began loudly. 'Me and me mum does our best. It ain't easy keepin' an eye on the little bleeders.'

Heads nodded knowingly, and the lumpy, shapeless woman squealed encouragement: 'You tell 'em, gal!'

Geed up by her mum, she struggled to put her feelings into words. It all came gushing out.

'I been campaigning for a year, ain't I? Sent letters to *The News*. Kept on at the coppers: fat lot o' good that did, din' it? Even wrote to the Council . . . They done bugger all!'

The word got the response intended. A great roar of approval. Kids cheered, not knowing what she was on about, but enjoying the way she said it.

'Tell 'em, gal!' came the shriek again.

'I knows where one of the bastards lives, I do. And I'm saying now, loud and clear: if nuffin's done to evict 'im, I'll go round and do 'im over meself!'

We all laughed and grinned at that. It was all good fun.

Elated by her own words, the angry woman suddenly dropped her guard and gave a broad, gap-toothed grin.

No doubt she'd never addressed a crowd before. I felt proud of her; it takes guts to stand up and talk like that.

She had no idea what she was starting!

Fascists

Some of the papers I delivered next morning had pictures of our soapbox woman on the front page. 'Vigilante', one called her, whatever that meant. Well, at least she'd pushed me and Mum off the pages of the local rag.

'Thank goodness for that,' was Mum's verdict, wiping her brow. 'She's welcome to it with her big mouth. They'll love her.'

'Are you jealous, Mum?' I asked.

She laughed at that. 'Oh yeah! But she's got guts, I'll give her that.'

'What's a vigilante?' I asked. Mum knew these things.

'You talking about her? Oh, so that's what they're calling her, eh? I can think of better names. Vigilante—someone who keeps watch against danger, self-appointed usually.'

'Two of her kids go to our school,' I added; 'one's in Marko's gang.'

'She's certainly got her hands full,' remarked Mum. 'I don't envy her. She must be on the welfare fiddle.'

Five kids wasn't a big deal round our way. Some girls got themselves up the spout straight from school. They knew Welfare would take care of them, even if the fathers didn't.

One kid and you got looked after, with a flat and that. Two kids brought an extra bedroom—but only if one was a girl and one a boy. Three was a house with three bedrooms, and so on. The more kids you had the bigger the house—as well as all your bills taken care of.

Some kids at school would boast about cheating the System.

Getting stuff on mail order that you never paid for . . .

Going 'shopping' with prams and pushchairs in department stores—they never took mothers to court for nicking goods. All they did was ban you—so you 'shopped' in other centres and nearby towns.

Getting social security even when a kid's dad lived in the house. Sometimes this welfare bloke would hang about outside with his camera, trying to get evidence. But so many were at it that the 'Neighbourhood Watch' gave plenty of warning.

Working the Welfare was a way of life on our estate. You never answer the door without peeking from an upstairs window first. So when our doorbell went that Saturday morning, we jumped guiltily. Not that Mum was on the fiddle, even if she did rely on child support.

'Could be your Big Moment, Mum,' I teased her. 'Ms Jeanette Goodall, *This is Your Life!*'

'Oh, go on with you,' she said. 'Go and see who it is while I tidy up.'

When I opened the door, I got a shock. I recognized him at once, even though he now wore a brown jacket and white shirt. It was our RAP man.

'Is Mrs Goodall in?' he asked politely.

'*Ms* Goodall,' I corrected him.

He frowned, but made the change, 'Ms Goodall. Can I see her? My name's Jeffrey.'

I wasn't sure whether that was his first or his second name. But I shouted for Mum.

'Mu-u-m! There's a bloke for you!'

'OK, coming,' came a distant voice.

'Hold on,' I said, leaving the door ajar. 'She won't be a mo'.'

I returned to my cello. I'd promised Sanjeev a cello

recital at eleven; it made up for banning him from my paper round. As Mr Wimbush said, 'It's good experience to play before an audience.' Even an audience of one!

I heard noises below as Mum showed the visitor into the tidied-up living room. Soon the voices gave way to a rattle of cups and whistle of kettle. I guessed she was making him a cup of coffee, with some broken digestives. After that I forgot all about them as I concentrated on my music. Then Sanjeev arrived and came straight up; I sat him down and treated him to scales and exercises.

After several minutes, the strangest racket came bounding up the stairs. It was so loud I couldn't focus on my playing. Sanjeev and I went to investigate at the top of the stairs. Whatever was going on?

'Don't you come here with your nasty propaganda!' Mum was shouting.

'Mark my words,' the man replied loudly. 'Perverts are just the tip of the iceberg. They're all scum—perverts, homosexuals, communists, blacks . . . '

'Get out of my house,' screamed Mum. 'Take your filth back to Nazi Germany!'

'Hitler knew how to cleanse society,' the man bawled back. 'With the gas chambers!'

Mum needed help. Hold on, Mum, the cavalry are coming!

Sanjeev and I rode down the stairs on our white chargers to the rescue. We weren't needed. The old skinhead, his shaven dome very red, was on his way out. One look at us two kids told him all.

'I should've known it,' he flung at Mum. 'A den of half-castes!'

He marched down the passage and out of the door, trying to hold on to his dignity. It wasn't easy with Mum in enraged pursuit. She stood in the doorway, screaming abuse at him as he slid into his car and drove off.

'Fascist! Racist pig!'

Paddy joined in with some insults of his own. No man would get the better of the Deadly Duo!

It took two cups of coffee and Sanjeev's presence before I dared ask Mum what had happened. Half to herself, she mumbled, 'All sorts jump on the bandwagon, just waiting their chance to exploit the situation . . . ' Turning to me, she said seriously, 'That, son, was a British patriot, so-called. A member of the British National Party—in other words, a fascist. Any opportunity to peddle their vile creed. To him all gays are paedophiles preying on little children. If he had his way he'd gas them all.'

Sanjeev and I exchanged anxious glances. It was getting more and more difficult to understand.

Abuse

We had the eerie feeling that the eyes of the country, if not the world, were on our estate. Every day at JG's, a crowd gathered to scan the papers. People changed the habit of a lifetime, buying newspapers they'd never dreamed of reading before—just for pictures and stories of the 'Protest'.

Women and children demand action!

'Out the sex beasts!' say residents!

Toddlers cry 'Hang 'em!'

Like a swarm of flies round a dustbin, those reporters were everywhere, taking photos, flashing fivers and tenners for anyone who'd spin them a tale.

Many did. Not only protesters. The papers vied with one another for the most 'newsworthy' story. Most reporters regarded us as ignorant morons, good for a laugh—and we went along with it. I don't think they realized we were conning them. Maybe they didn't care as long as the story was good copy.

One boy I knew played one journalist off against another, holding out for the highest bid. His story even made it to page 2. He laid it on good and thick.

'I was walking along mindin' me business, see. And this old geezer comes out and says "Gi's a 'and with the dustbin, son. I got a gammy 'and." So I goes in to do a good turn when three other geezers jump out and lock me in. Then they goes and makes me watch this dirty video. I cries and struggles, but one holds a carving knife and threatens to slit me throat. After that they turns on me, don't they. Three of 'em holds me down and strips me bollock naked, while the other one does 'orrible fings to me. Too 'orrible to tell yer.

'No, I don't go and tell me mum. No, I don't go to the coppers—what bleedin' good would that do? Doctor? Waffor? They're all bent anyway. Can't even speak English proper. Anyway, those filthy perverts says they'll do me in if I grasses on 'em.'

He got fifty quid for his story. Then he went and sold it to a weekly magazine—for seventy. As Mum said, he was laughing all the way to the bank.

Those papers, they'll print anything to sell more copies. They certainly didn't give a thought to me carrying them in my bag each morning!

Every evening you had a big crowd of people, mainly women and children, parading up and down Allaway Avenue with slogans scrawled on bits of plywood or old sheets. Usually it was that spiky-haired woman—the one with the biggest lip—leading the parade.

And every evening, the TV cameras were on hand to show the nation what the residents thought about perverts. Maybe they hoped someone might spice up the reports, what with their face on telly for the first time. Well, they were in luck.

At first it was a bit of a laugh. But gradually it turned nasty, especially when the police tried to butt in. Someone walloped a copper over the head with a wooden banner, screaming abuse at him. You'd have thought the sight of a policeman covered in blood would have calmed them

84

down. Just the opposite. They were like animals scenting blood.

A stander-by, one of the few blokes who'd bothered turning out, sprang forward to 'defend our women'; he started punching another copper and broke his nose. There were these women, urging him on, 'Go on, do the swine! Smash 'is face in!'

Not nice at all. Nasty.

I didn't go down to the Green after that.

'What makes people act like animals?' I asked Mum.

'That's a lesson for you,' she said. 'You see what can happen when people feel strongly about something; they join together and get carried away, drunk on their own power.'

'But tiny tots are screaming and swearing at the police,' I said. 'And their mums urge them on.'

'One starts, others follow. Not just kids. It's like a herd of buffalo: one panics and rushes off madly, and all the rest follow, not knowing why or where.'

'She's such a big mouth,' I said, thinking of the 'vigilante' woman. 'She just shouts her mouth off, swearing in front of the kids, any old words to stir people up.'

'Steady on, son,' cried Mum from the kitchen. 'Don't be too hard on her. Sure she's got a big mouth. I know a little bit about her; we were at school together, Tracy and I. You have to understand why people do what they do.'

She dried her hands, then came and sat next to me.

'Now, listen, Tom. I don't want you repeating this, OK? I've always been frank with you. I want you to understand a bit about mob psychology. It all started when she was about five: her grandad, her dad's dad, used to cuddle her, only he didn't stop at cuddles, if you know what I mean. That went on for years and she was too scared to tell a soul; she bottled it up inside her. It's still

85

there. Really messed up her life. She became such a tearaway that her mum had to put her into care. And what happened? Like many kids in care, she suffered more abuse. She got pregnant at sixteen. Then she shacked up with a drug addict until he landed in the loony bin, out of his skull on drugs. He left her with three more kids. Now she's got five, the last one from a student she took in while he was over here. But he shoved off, leaving her in the lurch.'

Mum sighed: woman-to-woman sympathy. 'Not a pretty story, is it?' she said. 'Now you know why she's angry, hitting out at men and the world that have let her down, abused her, exploited her. Yes, she's wrong-headed in what she's doing. She's seduced by the TV cameras; and she's playing into the hands of the bigots and the gutter press. But she needs our pity, not our scorn.'

You live and learn. It was hard to take in, especially as a boy. But after that I looked at Mum's schoolfriend through different eyes.

The Cello

It was the day of the audition. Terry Wimbush arrived at our house bright and early; we were to have a quick run-through. That done, we—Mum, Mr Wimbush, and I—took the train for Winchester at nine-thirty.

In my pocket I carried a Good Luck card from Sanjeev. It was addressed 'To My Boy Friend, Tom'. Whether that was his awkward English or sloppy writing I don't know. Not that it mattered. The card was meant for my eyes only and to wish me well.

A few weeks back, he'd showed me a story he'd written. It was called 'The Cello'. Very moving: all about a cello who falls in love with a trombone. They used to play sad songs to each other, telling of their love. One day, a spiteful bassoon overheard their duet and told the rest of the orchestra. The violins tittered, the trumpets blared, the kettledrum banged on, the clarinets jeered. All because they were from different sections of the orchestra! The cello was strings and the trombone brass. So, although they made the most beautiful music, everyone sneered and called them names.

Sanjeev hadn't finished his story; he just showed it to me for my reaction.

'Wicked,' I said to encourage him.

'Do you think I ought to hand it in?' he asked gravely.

'Don't see why not,' I said. 'I'd give it top marks. It's very moving.'

So he did. And the teacher liked it so much he read it out in class. Big mistake! If the English teacher didn't see through it, some of the class did. After that, boys would taunt Sanjeev with trombone actions and bending over to show him their backsides. Marko's mob tied me into the 'joke', doing cello imitations with one hand and wanker gestures with the other.

If anyone had forgotten my 'prize performance', Sanjeev's story brought it back with a vengeance. Not only was I a 'cissy' and a 'nancy boy'; I was now an 'arse bandit'. There's nothing bullies love more than picking on someone weak and soft. Even though I was a year younger than Sanjeev, I was capable of standing up for myself—my football mates helped. But Sanjeev was alone and, being Asian, he got double taunts: 'Paki' and 'faggot'.

I think the taunts reached Mum's ears, but she kept quiet about them. She'd always said I had to fight my own battles. And so I did on the football pitch and cello. Recently, I'd had enough on my plate what with the audition, so I was able to push the bullying to the back of my mind.

Well, there we were, the three of us, on our way to Winchester. Despite the audition, the events of recent days weren't far from our thoughts. Perhaps to take my mind off the coming ordeal, Mum joked to Mr Wimbush, 'I haven't seen you marching on the Green.'

The joke fell flat. In hurt tones, Mr Wimbush said, 'No, but I've had a visit.'

Mum looked puzzled. 'What d'you mean?'

'Oh, some yobs shouting abuse, spraying my front door, pushing little gifts of dog dirt through the letterbox.'

Mum and I stared at him.

'What for? Who'd want to do that?' said Mum, unable to take it in.

'What for?' he repeated. 'God knows. I hate paedophiles as much as the next man. But once the hounds are set loose, baying for blood, anyone "different" is fair game.'

'But . . . people *know* you; they *like* you,' said Mum.

'Look, Jeanette,' he said helplessly. 'I'm a "queen" to many people. I know they snigger behind my back. I don't mind. Sticks and stones and all that . . . But when the mob rules, all sorts of innocent folk suffer.'

'It's becoming a witch hunt,' said Mum angrily, her face turning red. 'Can't you tell the police or the local paper?'

He laughed bitterly. 'I did mention it to a bobby, someone I've known for years. But he said it was *my* look-out. "Queers get what they deserve," were his exact words. As for the papers, why should they care? The longer this goes on, the more papers they sell. Profit. That's all they're bothered about. Not truth. Not justice. Not queer-bashing . . . '

We spent the remainder of the journey staring out of the window, thinking our own thoughts. I have to confess, I soon replaced Mr Wimbush's troubles with my own musical worries. I examined my left-hand finger pads, pressed imaginary strings up and down the armrest, checked my chunk of resin, hummed 'Ave Maria' under my breath and dreamed of fame: playing Elgar or Dvořák at the Guildhall before a packed audience.

My actions and expressions must have taken Mr Wimbush out of his gloomy thoughts. For he suddenly burst out laughing.

'Tom, you have the Gift. You *live* music. Your whole body is playing even when you've no cello between your knees. One day you'll be a world-famous cellist. And I'll be at every concert—if I can afford it.'

'I'll get free tickets,' I said with a grin. 'For you and Mum.'

The Audition

Quite a setting. As big as a football pitch. The Great Hall smelt of old timbers and dusty floorboards, rather like Nelson's flagship, the *Victory*, in Portsmouth dockyard. And it hummed: with chattering youngsters all done up in their Sunday best, nervous mums, dads, and tutors speaking too loudly, dark-suited judges bustling between all four corners of the hall.

We were early. After queuing up to register and learn my allotted time—11.45—we had a good hour to kill.

'Let's make the most of it now we're here,' said Mum. 'Great opportunity for a history lesson.'

Good old Mum. Never one to let a chance slip for improving my mind. Even on a Saturday. I have to admit the place was *wicked*, like a medieval banqueting hall, with high-up stained glass windows and dark oak panelling all round.

'Let's take a look at the Round Table,' said Mum.

Our footsteps echoed hollowly on the wooden floor as we headed for a distant corner of the hall. Halfway up the wall was a massive round table, rather like one of those roulette tables in a casino—not that I'd ever seen one in the flesh.

'Is this really King Arthur's Round Table?' I asked in awe.

'Some say so,' said Mum guardedly. 'It was dug up years ago. King Arthur and his knights could well have had their castle here.'

I was imagining Sir Lancelot and Sir Galahad sitting at the Table, next to Arthur and his wife, the fair Queen

Guinevere. Those were the great doors through which the Green Knight rode on his green horse, throwing down a challenge to Sir Gawain . . . Wow! And I'd be playing in this very hall whose walls echoed to the music of Arthur's Court.

Mr Wimbush went and spoiled it.

'Some say the table dates from much later; it's a copy of the genuine article.'

Seeing my disappointment, he added, 'What's for certain is that Sir Walter Raleigh was sentenced here and Bloody Judge Jeffreys held his Assizes in this very hall in the late seventeenth century. This is where he sentenced several hundred people to death and a thousand others to slavery on American plantations.'

Now that's history I enjoyed! I decided I'd be Judge Jeffreys when I gave my audition. I'd give them what for. If they didn't like it . . . 'Off with their heads!'

When it came to it, I felt more like his victims, quaking in my boots—if they wore boots in those days.

I was sitting among the budding cellists in the Round Table sector, waiting for my name to be called. It was a bit like the kick-in before a football match, where you size up the opposition and see they're all bigger and cleverer than you. One lad even wore a bow tie and gave a bow before he played. Not that that prevented him from fluffing some notes.

When my name was called, Mum squeezed my hand as I stood up and walked forward to the front. I sat in the 'hot seat' with my back to the crowd and my face to the three judges: two men and a woman. No one smiled encouragement. They looked dead bored. An old fellow peered at me over the top of his half-moon specs.

'Thomas,' he said, 'we want you to play the scale of F major, then the two exercises on the stand before you. Finally, your free piece.'

91

He gave a superior smile to the others and cracked a joke. 'You'd better tell us what it is in case we don't recognize it.'

No one laughed.

In a squeaky voice, I said, ' ''Ave Maria'', Schubert.'

(Note: practise low, husky voice more!)

I made myself as comfy as I could. But this was so new and strange. For a start, there was no one to focus on but these three wise monkeys. And the racket! From the other three corners came squeaks and groans, trills and burps as violas, violins, and double basses went through their paces.

To cap it all, halfway through the first exercise, the Town Hall clock chimed out,

PLAY UP, POMPEY. POMPEY, PLAY UP!
PLAY UP, POMPEY. POMPEY, PLAY UP!
DONG-G-G!

Twelve times.

I could hardly hear myself play. Yet, though I was now more annoyed than nervous, the chimes cheered me up. And I reckon I played 'Ave Maria' better than ever.

'Thank you, Thomas,' said the bespectacled gentleman. 'You outchimed the chimes. Next. Eunice Wilson.'

I shuffled off, as relieved as anyone escaping the dentist's chair. But I needed reassurance badly.

'How was I, Mum?'

'Not for me to say,' she said unhelpfully.

'What did *you* think, Mr Wimbush?' I asked.

'A trifle fast in the opening passage of the ''Ave'',' he said thoughtfully. 'And you dropped a clanger when the clock clanger clanged!' He giggled at his own joke. 'You were fine, Tom. Just fine.'

His broad smile was all the encouragement I needed.

Name and Shame

A few days after my Round Table recital, we had a visitor. It was too early for the coalman and too late for the postman. A smell of garden roses wafted beneath my nose all the way from the front door. And outside our gate I could see a smart new Renault Laguna glinting in the sun. If that weren't enough, a loud voice broke the morning calm.

'Hi there! Ms Goodall? Jeanette Goodall? Great! Emma Cliveden. From London. Journalist?'

She spoke as if she was an old chum. Only the last word registered with Mum. What with the audition and protests, the promised interview had slipped her mind.

'Oh, er, yes, do come in,' she said in a put-on posh voice. 'I wasn't expecting you.'

'No peace for the wicked. Morning, afternoon, and night. Seven days a week . . . '

The woman wittered on like a lavatory brush salesperson. I had no time for a disappearing act; my escape route was cut off. But I was intrigued to see the owner of the loud voice.

'This is my son, Tom,' said Mum, ushering the visitor into our front room, clearly glad of an ally.

She was youngish, smart-looking, but plastered in make-up—rather like a clown's face, very pale with a scarlet gash for a mouth.

'Hi there, Tom,' she barked, as if shouting to a dog in a field. 'Great to meet you.'

She strode across the room as I stood up, and held out a surprisingly dainty hand. While Mum was shooing

Paddy out of the back door, I hesitated, unused to shaking hands. I assumed I had to shake it, not bite it off. A limp handshake left me smelling like a fresh grave at a funeral.

But I was soon discarded in favour of our settee and a black leather bag was dumped on the carpet. Out came a thick notepad and Mont Blanc ballpen.

'Now, let's get down to business,' she said briskly.

Mum was ill at ease. Visitors had to drink tea or coffee before business. Even the rent man had to have a cuppa; it was only fit and proper.

'Oh, go on then,' the Emma woman finally agreed at the third time of asking. 'A dash of milk, skimmed, no sugar.'

Mum's labours in the kitchen left me at the reporter's mercy. I was busy sneaking a sniff of my right perfumed hand when she turned her pretty brown eyes on me.

'Now, Tony,' she said, 'what do you think of all the kerfuffle?'

I didn't know what 'Tony' or 'kerfuffle' meant. It was only when Mum corrected the mistake from the kitchen that the woman on the settee changed tack.

'He's Tom,' Mum sang out.

'Oh, good gracious me. I'm awfully sorry, young man,' she said with real pain in her eyes. 'Tom, Tom, the piper's son! It's a terrible business, isn't it?'

Seeing no gleam of recognition in my eyes, she spelled it out.

'What happened to that poor little girl. You must feel proud of the protesters, eh?'

I wasn't sure what to say except 'Yeah'.

'How about you, Tom, have you taken part?'

Desperately I looked towards the door. Come on, Mum! Teaspoons rattled in saucers, tray clattered on the formica top. Mum wasn't ready yet.

'I went down to the Green on the first day.'

'What? Right.' She scribbled away on her pad in some secret code. 'What do you think about it, Tom?'

I stalled for time.

'I guess-ss, umm, something ought to be done. Well, I mean, umm, no one likes paedophiles, do they?'

'Do you know of any round here, Tom?'

She asked her question without looking up, then sat silent, awaiting my answer.

'I've heard of one.'

To fill the long gap, I had to talk some more, while she scribbled on.

'A guy called Victor Burnett. They want him sent packing. I know people have been on at him. I dunno. He seems harmless enough . . . I just dunno.'

'Is that Burnett with one or two t's?' she said, looking up.

'Three teas,' announced Mum, appearing with a trayful of three cups, teapot, and saucer of ginger crunch biscuits. 'But two t's in Burnett.'

The journalist sat with pen poised over notepad. At last, the penny dropped and she said, 'Oh, yar, funny.'

She didn't smile. But, luckily for me, she turned her attention on Mum.

'I read your piece in *The News*. Super. You favour full disclosures, I take it.'

'Yes and no,' said Mum boldly. 'In some countries, the local welfare office delivers leaflets to residents when a convicted paedophile moves into the area. That could be beneficial to both sides. If a bloke's done his time, he deserves a second chance—and he has to live somewhere. It can put people's minds at rest, stops rumours spreading, if they know what's what.'

'Do *you* know of any paedophiles hereabouts?' said the clown-mask lady, sipping her tea and declining the offer of a biscuit.

95

'Not really,' said Mum. 'That's what I mean. There are lots of rumours flying about, protesters can make an innocent person's life a misery.'

Perhaps Mum was thinking of Terry Wimbush.

The journalist had gone quiet again.

'All I've *heard*,' continued Mum, 'is that two innocent families have been hounded from their homes, while an ex-con has gone to ground till the storm blows over. We have a gay friend who's had to put up with a heap of abuse. Someone was saying that another man was targeted because he lives alone with his mother. That can't be right, can it?'

'Oh dear, how really awful!' said Emma Cliveden, her forehead cracking with the strain of a concerned frown. 'Do you know, Jeanette, I heard of a crowd in Gwent that attacked a paediatrician's surgery by mistake!'

She found that funny. Mentally I noted the word to ask Mum about later. It gave me an opportunity to escape.

'Must do my practice,' I said apologetically. 'Please excuse me.'

She was very polite, getting up to shake hands again and asking me what I played. She turned out to be a cellist herself. 'Lapsed,' she said: 'No time these days.'

A nice woman. Smelt delicious too.

She and Mum seemed to get on like a house on fire, chatting merrily away for another forty minutes or so. Finally, she excused herself. 'I've got to squeeze in a swift chat with your RAP leader.'

As she was leaving, she called up the stairs to say goodbye. But she was halfway through the door by the time I rushed out to the landing. I was just in time to see her hand Mum a white envelope with the words, 'For you and Tony, with the compliments of the newspaper.'

And she was gone. Clip-clop. Zoom!

When I went downstairs, Mum was sitting on the settee, mumbling to herself, 'A hundred pounds! What for? Hundred smackers . . .'

Fame

I didn't deliver papers on a Sunday. But Mr Gant unexpectedly rang up with an urgent message.

'I think you ought to read the nation's No. 1 Sunday,' he said breathlessly. 'It's got a bit on you and your mother.'

I was round JG's like a shot. Under strict instructions to bring the paper home right away—so that Mum could read it first—I squeezed it under my arm and cycled home. From what I could see, the front page was all photos, like a rogues' gallery. Probably candidates for next England football manager.

Mum's thoughts were far from football. One glance and she collapsed in a heap on the settee. Now and again, as her eyes darted across, up and down, she uttered a word: 'What! How! Me?'

In the end, she dropped the paper on the floor and rushed off to the kitchen. I could tell she was stressed out. Not only was she as red as a postbox, she always made a cup of tea to calm herself down. While she was out of the room, I spread the paper over the carpet.

The photos were *not* of the new football manager. They were prison pictures, front and side: of three men, all desperadoes by the look of them. Unshaven, snarling, evil. Two giant words stood above the photos:

NAME SHAME

Beneath each picture was a name with age. The first was Victor Burnett!

98

Under the headline *'Name and Shame'* was an article by 'Our Special Correspondent' Emma Cliveden. The roses lady in the clown mask! From what I could make out, it talked a lot of 'time to'—protect our kids, 'out' convicted paedophiles, act decisively, follow the estate's example . . . 'Time to . . . (see pages 2 and 3)'.

When I turned the page, I got a shock. Two more photos: me and Mum in a cuddle, and Mum's schoolfriend Tracy—the same ones that had appeared in *The News*. Under the sub-heading 'Mother and Son Speak Out', the paper said:

> Young Tom Goodall, 13, names pervert Victor Burnett. The cello-playing schoolboy wants his kind kicked out of the neighbourhood . . . Jeanette Goodall, a 34-year-old single mother, agrees with her son: 'Time for the Council to act,' says Jeanette, an attractive redhead. 'Let us know where the perverts live and we'll deal with them . . . ' Her old school pal, Tracy O'Connell, feisty leader of Residents Against Paedophiles, demands action to clear the streets of monsters who prey on little children . . .

The article went on to assure readers that the newspaper would stand up for the concerned parents and everyone like them. It would be running a 'NAME AND SHAME!' campaign until Government acted 'to stamp this evil out!'

With Mum still in the kitchen, I idly turned the pages, looking at pictures of film stars and pop singers, as well as young girl 'hopefuls' in skimpy swimsuits and a 'saucy pair' baring their boobs.

Normally Mum never allowed the paper in the house. So I took the chance to improve my education.

No sooner had I put down the paper than the phone rang. It was Auntie Di. She and Mum gassed for half an hour, with Mum angry and spitting out words like 'cynical', 'hypocrites', 'lies', and 'manipulation'. I assumed she was referring to the article.

The phone didn't stop ringing all morning and afternoon. Some calls were from reporters wanting 'quotes'. She told them to 'go to hell!'

Once the phone cooled down, another noise took its place: the blare of police car sirens. It started soon after tea and carried on till gone midnight. We were too scared to go out to investigate.

'I hope that rag is pleased with what it's done,' Mum muttered. 'Just listen to that racket. That's mob rule for you, stupid people whipped into a frenzy by unscrupulous journalists. Where *will* it lead?'

The racket certainly made up Mum's mind about one thing. We were not going to buy a new bow for my cello after all. She poked the banknotes back into the envelope, checked the paper's address and wrote it on the letter.

'They needn't think they can buy me with their filthy lucre!' she shouted.

'What's filthy lucre, Mum?' I asked innocently.

'Dirty money!' she cried.

Now, a hundred pounds was not to be sneezed at in our house. And I wanted to know why Mum was sending it back. Maybe I could change her mind.

'That lady gave the money for you, Mum,' I said. 'You know, like you give someone a tip for being helpful. You deserve it.'

That only made her worse. I could see the new bow disappearing with every word.

'I wouldn't dream of taking their handouts,' she growled. 'Tom, let me ask you this: what would you think of someone who says they want to protect under-age children, yet shows off half-naked sixteen-year-old girls?'

'It's what you call "cynical", I guess,' I said.

'That's the word, son. That woman who came here lives by peddling trash. She's not interested in the truth or in us; she *uses* us to give her nasty story the ring of truth. Her ill-gotten gains depend on how many extra papers her story will sell. And I've fallen into her trap by buying an extra copy!'

The phone saved me from returning the paper to the newsagent and demanding Mum's money back . . .

'Who the hell's that at this time of night?' Mum exploded. 'If it's another reporter I'll give them a flea in their ear!'

It wasn't a journalist. It was the police. I saw Mum go pale and her hands tremble. In a shaky voice, she was asking, 'When? Where? How is he?'

She put down the receiver with a bang. Turning to me, she said in a choking voice, 'They've torched Terry's house. He's badly burned.' She started crying.

Instead of calming her down, I made it worse by my questions.

'How is he? Where is he?'

Through her tears she muttered, 'It's touch and go. He's in the QA. Maybe we'll go tomorrow.'

I'm sure she blamed herself for the tragedy.

101

News Good and Bad

It's odd how news comes in pairs: good and bad.

Next morning I had a letter bearing the Winchester crest. While Mum was busy burning the toast, I snaffled my letter from a pile of junk mail and escaped with it upstairs.

Sitting on my unmade bed, I tore the envelope open and pulled the pages out, face down. I tried the guessing game. What did the contents tell?

For a start, there wasn't just a single page—brief rejection? There were two stiffish sheets, one bearing three or four paragraphs, one a list of dates. My hopes rose. Surely *good* news.

Unable to sustain the suspense, I turned the first page over and read with bated breath.

Dear Master Goodall,

We are pleased to inform you of your audition success in violin/viola/violoncello/double bass.

You are accordingly accepted as member of the County Youth Orchestra. Your acceptance must be regarded as conditional upon prompt and regular attendance at rehearsals.

Please note the enclosed times and dates of rehearsals to be held in the Great Hall.

Congratulations,

Yours faithfully,

Geo. K. Fry B.Mus., FRSA

My first thought was to phone Mr Wimbush with the news. My heart sank to my boots as I remembered last night's terrible news. At least it would cheer him up—if he was in a fit state to hear it.

'Breakfast!'

Defying Mum's house rules, I ran downstairs and rattled the kitchen table.

'Don't run. Walk!' she shouted with her back to me. 'Any post?'

'The usual,' I replied matter-of-factly. 'But *I* had a letter.'

She whipped round, dripping porridge all over the floor.

'What? From Winchester?'

'Yep. I'm in.'

Normally, she'd be jumping for joy. This is what I'd worked for—one step more than she'd ever achieved. But her eyes were still red from crying.

'It'll give Mr Wimbush a lift,' I said.

'Maybe,' she murmured, on her knees wiping up the mess. 'I rang earlier, there's no change. No visitors yet. "Ring back later," the nurse said.'

When Mum was down, she didn't collapse in a helpless heap; she got punchy, spoiling for a fight. I guessed what was going through her mind, but I had to tread carefully.

'Penny for your thoughts, Mum.'

'Nothing,' she mumbled to herself. Then, as if cross with herself for excluding me, she said, 'Why? He wouldn't harm a fly. Sure, people made fun of him. But they liked him, respected him; he was always kind and helpful, cheered you up when you were down in the dumps.'

She looked so helpless, my mum, with her watery eyes, freckled nose, pale face, and straggly marmalade hair. But lovely—with a natural beauty—even when upset. A

103

thousand times prettier than that fancy journalist with her face caked in muck.

'Have they caught anyone?' I asked, probing deeper.

'Not that I know of,' she replied.

Her face and tone were on the turn—from docile pussycat to menacing tiger.

'But . . . I'm going . . . to . . . find . . . out. And when I do, God help them . . .'

She sprang up and padded, tiger-like, towards the phone. I heard her leafing through pages, picking up the receiver and dialling a number. Then her voice, hard and threatening, said loudly, 'Is that Tracy O'Connell? Her mother? It's Jeanette Goodall. Fetch your daughter, will you!' A short wait, then, 'Tracy! This is Jeanette Goodall. Yes, that's right. Did you hear about Terry Wimbush?' (Pause) 'No use being sorry now, is it! Who did it?' (Pause) *What?!* You're not serious! Oh, my God!'

The growls and snarls continued for a couple of minutes, but they gradually died down. I heard my name mentioned and, for some odd reason, Sanjeev's. What on earth had he got to do with it? Finally, the phone clicked and Mum returned, looking more like a scared rabbit than a fierce tiger. I'd never seen her so upset.

'What's up, Mum?' I dared ask.

'Tracy reckons your friend Sanjeev's brothers may have done it. Police are questioning them now.'

'I don't believe it!' I cried. 'They don't even know Mr Wimbush.'

'Maybe not.'

'It's all a plot to shift the blame on to Asians,' I decided.

'I'm sure some would like to think so,' said Mum, a troubled look in her eyes. 'But Tracy says Sanjeev's mother found a letter in her son's pocket. Do you know anything about that?'

I froze. A letter? Oh no, not another *love* letter!

'No,' I said miserably. 'But it wouldn't be the first.'

'I think you'd better tell me about it,' said Mum quietly.

Confession

My confession to Mum was the worst moment of my life. I told her all about Sanjeev's letter, his 'Cello' story and his Good Luck card. She listened, her face drawn, not interrupting. At the end, she took my hand in hers and said with a sigh, 'Thank you, Tom. And how do you feel about him?'

'I don't love him as he loves me,' I said nervously. 'It's hard to put into words.'

'Try,' she said softly, encouraging me with a squeeze. 'I'm your mother. I'm not going to laugh or cry or shout at you. I want to help.'

'He's my best friend,' I murmured. 'I'm fond of him. He's so kind and unselfish. When he listens to me play, he's just happy for me, proud of me, he doesn't think of himself.'

'And how do *you* feel?'

'I don't know. Sometimes I tell myself it's a passing phase, part of growing up and stuff. I'll grow out of it and be like everybody else. Yet . . . something inside me tells me I *am* different, I'm *not* like everyone else. There are times when I'd like to hold his hand, even kiss him. That's not natural, Mum, is it?'

'Depends what you call natural,' she said with a slight smile. 'Some of us are born one way, so it's *natural* for boy to love girl, or girl boy. Some of us, though, are born another way where it's *natural* for boy to love boy, or girl to love girl. That's nature. We're all different.'

I'd never discussed this with anyone before, never dared. I'd intended to talk to Terry Wimbush, but hadn't

106

got round to it. But Mum? I'd been so scared of hurting her. Yet now that it was out I felt *gi-normously* relieved.

'Lots of people are gay,' said Mum, 'in all walks of life—even your footballers. You can't always tell by looking at them. Some hide it, use marriage as a cover. They're the ones to feel sorry for. Scientists reckon between five and ten per cent of the population in every country is either gay or bisexual.'

I tried to get my head round that, picturing my class at school, my football team, the auditioning kids. So one in ten or twenty kids was gay!

Teachers! Footballers! Girls! It was mind-boggling. I wasn't alone, after all . . .

'But not many show it, not so's you'd know,' I said, thinking of school.

'I guess not,' said Mum. 'What would happen if you stood up in class and said: "I'm gay!"?'

I had to laugh at that. I could just imagine my friends' faces.

'Some'd be embarrassed. Some probably wouldn't know what I was on about. Some'd take the mickey. And the bullies would make my life a misery, like they did with David and Sanjeev.'

'It isn't easy being gay,' said Mum sympathetically. 'Anyone who's different can suffer: different colour, different religion, different hair, fat or skinny, short or lanky. In Nazi Germany, Jews, gypsies, communists, and homosexuals were all sent to the gas chambers— because they were different. That should have taught the world a lesson about prejudice. Slowly but surely understanding is growing. There have been openly gay ministers in government—and that's never happened before.'

I thought about that. You didn't have to act the fool like some camp comedians on telly to get fame. You could be

Prime Minister, sportsman, composer, actor, even cellist! Anything you like.

'The important thing is to be respected for what you *do*, not what you *are*—straight, gay, or in the middle.'

'Thanks, Mum,' I said. 'I'm ever so glad I talked to you. Are you shocked?'

'Goodness, no!' she exclaimed, getting up for another cup of tea. 'I've known for ages . . . '

What! Isn't that typical! She knew all along! Mum knows everything, even the darkest secrets.

'Tom,' she said with a change of tone, 'I have a question; and I want a straight answer.'

She looked me in the eyes and said, 'Did you and Sanjeev ever discuss this with Terry Wimbush?'

'*Never!*' I said.

'Did he know about you and Sanjeev?'

'If he did, he never let on. Why?'

'It seems Sanjeev's family thinks it was Terry who put you up to it, corrupted their son—and you too!'

'But that's loopy!'

I couldn't get my head round it. I trusted Sanjeev: he wouldn't have lumped any blame on Mr Wimbush. But . . . Terry Wimbush shopped at their store. He stood out like a sore thumb—a 'queen', as he put it himself. He taught me, all alone, in his house. He'd 'corrupted' me, and I'd 'corrupted' their son. It couldn't be *our* fault: we were too young to know any better . . .

'I blame it on all this scare-mongering,' said Mum, stirring her tea. 'Witch-hunts are bound to ensnare innocent victims. Well, now they've got a result, I hope they're satisfied!'

'What did your friend Tracy say?' I asked, eager to turn the heat off me.

'There was a near riot last night,' sighed Mum. 'People were that fired up by the papers. They torched cars and smashed shop windows—*any* cars, *any* windows. Some threw bricks at the police. Even tiny tots were kept up past midnight, screaming and swearing.'

'Isn't your friend just a little bit sorry about Mr Wimbush?'

'She reckons it's nothing to do with her. Says people like him get what they deserve—a "right bashing". She seemed to think it a good laugh: "Pakis bashing queers," to use her words.'

'Sanjeev's family is Indian,' I said.

'She wouldn't know the difference,' said Mum angrily.

She marched out with a red face to phone the hospital. It was a relief to hear her calm down quickly and mutter, 'Right, OK, after seven this evening then . . . Burns Unit. Ta.'

Clearly, Terry Wimbush was going to be all right.

Muggers

When I went to deliver the evening papers I saw the vandalism with my own eyes. Poor Mr Gant had had his windows smashed in; *and* his shop was trashed. It was the last straw.

'Bloody hooligans! Thirty-five years I've slaved in this shit-hole. And this is all the thanks I get. That's it: I'm getting out!'

He stood defeated, big wrinkled hands on the counter, speaking into the void, as if he had a customer before him.

'Pinched all me fags—and the dog meat!'

I found this so funny I blurted out, 'P'raps it was a smoking bulldog.'

He didn't see the joke. Didn't seem to hear me.

'I blame it on the weather, that global warming they're on about.' He rambled on, eyes staring into space. 'These hot sultry nights, they turn people queer. You always get riots of a warm summer's night. Nothing on telly, that's another factor . . . '

'What'll you do, Mr Gant?' I asked.

Slowly, like a robot, his head jerked my way. 'You still here? Get those papers out!'

Best to make myself scarce. Yet as I was going through the door, he muttered, 'I'll dig over me allotment, that's what I'll do. The Pakis can take over, like they have the fish and chip shop and the grocer's.'

'It's the Chinese that run the chippy,' I called back without waiting for a response. '*And* the Chinese takeaway.'

'Git!'

All along the main drag were burnt-out shells of cars, charred and blistery, some still smouldering. Phwoo-ar! The bitter stink of rubber and burnt treacle was so strong I had to put my shirt sleeve over my nose and mouth.

We don't have garages on the estate, so those with motor cars left them at the roadside, mostly old bangers. But they had been *somebody's* pride and joy. I suppose they'll wangle insurance out of the stingy companies— those that were insured, that is.

Throughout my round, neighbours were standing outside flats and houses, gabbing about last night's events. In a place where nothing much happened—if you leave out burglary, police swoops, vandalism, and wife-beating— 'Mob Run Riot' (as the paper's headline put it) was an EVENT.

What's more, it wasn't an *outside* event, it was our very own entertainment.

I was quite a celebrity—for all the wrong reasons.

'Hello, Tommy lad!'

'Well done, Master Goodall!'

'You done good, boy!'

All from people who'd never spoken to me before. But there was one discordant voice. A quietly-spoken elderly gentleman was waiting in his doorway as I passed; all I knew about him was that he was the sole morning *Guardian* amid the *Sun*s, *Mail*s, and *Mirror*s.

'I heard about your cello teacher,' he said quietly, as if not wanting to be overheard. 'I just wanted to say how sorry I am. A good man, very good man.'

'Thanks,' I said, hesitating at the next-door letterbox. 'Er, do you know Mr Wimbush?'

'Oh yes,' he said with a smile, 'I was once his English master, just after the war, down in Portsea. He got a scholarship to Oxford, you know . . . But he chose

111

to stay home and nurse his mother. A thoroughly decent sort.'

'I'll be seeing him at the Queen Alexandra later,' I said.

'Do give him my regards, will you. Mr Hitchens— "Scratch" Hitchens. Tell him this from me: *"Heaven has no rage, like love to hatred turned, Nor Hell a fury, like a woman scorned."* Will you remember that?'

'I think so, Mr Hitchens. Sorry, I must fly.' I gave him one back: 'Time and tide wait for no man. See ya.'

I was running late, what with all the unwanted attention. My admirers mostly seemed unsure whether to cheer or boo. Something was happening. No one knew what. Our patch had hit the national news. All Britain now knew of our estate. Was that good or bad?

Perhaps both. But it was too early to unravel good from evil.

SOMEONE, however, was in no doubt. And they were certainly bent on EVIL.

I'd almost completed my round—one more upstairs set of maisonette doors to go. I was just skipping down the stairwell when—*WHAM!* Something hit me in the stomach. I fell in a heap. If it hadn't been for my paper bag and four left-overs, I might have conked out.

Two brawny men stood over me, arms raised. From head to toe they were kitted out in black: commando balaclavas down to bovver boots. Both held baseball bats as if they were standing on strike base.

'Leave off!' I squealed. 'I've no money. Here, take my watch and papers . . . '

My only thought was that they were muggers.

One grunted, swung back the baseball bat and lammed into me. First the right arm, then the left. I heard a God-awful CRA-A-CK and felt a sharp pain shoot up my right arm. The noise seemed to satisfy them, for the hoods looked at each other, nodded and turned away. It was all over in a few seconds. Almost . . . One of the commando masks bent over my huddled form and snarled, 'Leave . . . Sanjeev . . . alone!'

And they were gone.

I waited until the clattering footsteps had faded away before trying to move. My legs were uninjured. My head was in one piece. My left arm was OK—thanks to the thick delivery bag.

But my guts were giving me gyp and my right arm . . . Oww-eee! Jesus, Mary, and Joseph! Now I knew what being blown up by a shell meant. One by one you tick off your body parts to see what's left. I was lucky. There were two pain spots: a broken arm and an aching belly.

I pulled myself up with my left hand and staggered back to JG's, dumped the bag in Mr Gant's shed and scooted home on my bike. At the door I collapsed into Mum's arms.

Hospital

We ended up at the hospital earlier than expected. Fortunately, it was only a ten minute walk from our house. After waiting in three separate queues for an hour and a half, I finally made it to X-ray; twenty minutes later a white-coat was pressing and pulling my arm to see how badly he could hurt me.

Squinting at my X-ray skeleton, he announced his diagnosis:

'Fracture of the lower humerus; possible radial nerve contusion with supracondylar abrasions.'

I'm not sure what language he was speaking, but he didn't hang around for a translation. The nurse who did the plaster cast was only slightly more forthcoming.

'It'll knit in six to eight weeks, *if* you keep it still. *No* football. *No* all-in wrestling, OK?'

'How about cello?' I asked seriously.

'Get away wid ya,' she said. 'No violent games at all!'

Bang went my rehearsals and the new football season.

Mum escorted me with my arm in a sling out of Casualty towards the Burns Unit; we stopped on the way for refreshment. I was in need of a hot drink, Mum was in need of serious interrogation.

'How *did* you do it?'

She obviously hadn't swallowed my tearful tale of tripping on the stone stairs.

'I told you, Mum.'

'Tom,' she said wearily, 'mothers have magical powers: they can see right into kids' minds. So don't lie to me. In

114

any case, with all this palaver, it's mighty coincidental that you fell and hurt yourself, wouldn't you say?'

I thought it over. I *knew* who had attacked me even though I'd never set eyes on them. If I didn't tell Mum, our mutual trust would be broken. She'd find out anyway by hook or by crook. She always did.

If I *did* tell her, there'd be hell to pay. Knowing Mum, she'd call the cops, we'd be up in court, me and Sanjeev would have to give evidence, and so on.

Trust *had* to come first.

'I didn't get a look at them,' I said, 'but I'm pretty sure who it was. Sanjeev's brothers. One said "Leave Sanjeev alone!" They came at me with baseball bats on a dark stairwell.'

'What idiots!' said Mum, spluttering on her cup of tea. 'They're already up for arson. Now this. But why go for your arms? Why not break your ribs, legs, kneecaps . . . ?'

It struck us both at the same time.

To stop me playing the cello!

'That cello is a symbol,' she decided. 'What they don't understand they try to destroy. First Terry, then you.'

'It's only a bit of old wood,' I muttered, wondering what she was talking about.

'Come on, son. We'll deal with that later. Let's get our visit over and done with.'

We made our way along corridors that went on forever; the vinyl floor was all shiny and speckled greeny-blue, like a running stream. Now and then notices signposted tributaries going off to right and left: Oncology, Paediatrics, Physiotherapy, Osteopathy, Chapel of Rest.

At last we came to plain old English: Burns Unit.

We were guided by Sister towards a stuffy, humid side-ward smelling strongly of steamed pudding. The hot air caught in throat and nostril.

At the door, Sister said severely, 'Get your coughing done here! Ten minutes, no more.'

We didn't think to ask which bed. There were four, each one set in a big open drum on wheels that could be turned at any angle. Luckily, names were written on charts upon the wall. Otherwise we couldn't have told one from the other.

T. WIMBUSH was first on the left.

No tell-tale clues marked the charts, just words: 'Intravenous fluids every four hours.' 'Blood pressure . . . Pulse . . . ,' Squiggles filled the gaps.

Mum sat down on the single chair, while I stood behind her. The figure in the bed was covered in a sort of white canopy—like Snow White in a glass case, but with linen for glass. Only the head and feet were visible, although it wasn't easy to tell which was which for white and black charred patches.

The figure lay quiet and still.

'Terry, it's Tom and Jeanette,' Mum whispered, head bent towards the pillow.

No reply.

'We've brought some flowers and grapes,' she said helplessly.

I could tell from her breaking voice that Mum was about to blubber. That was the last thing the patient needed. Almost without noticing, I squeezed her arm with my good hand and took over.

'Mr Wimbush, I got in! All thanks to you . . . Here's the letter in my hand.'

I waved it in the air to make a crackle.

An up and down moan came from the bed.

That really set Mum off. Big tears rolled down her cheeks. Yet she did her best to stifle the howls welling up inside her.

I babbled on, talking to thin air.

116

'I was on my paper round, see, this evening, up Allenby Terrace, and who d'you think I bumped into? He said he was an old teacher of yours: "Scratch" somebody. He said to give you his regards and tell you this . . . ' I racked my brain to get it right. ' *"Heaven has no rage, like love to hatred turned, Nor Hell a fury, like a woman scorned."* '

A gurgle trickled out from the pillow. It tried again and this time formed a word, 'Congreve.'

'Try not to talk, Terry,' said Mum earnestly. 'We'll come back tomorrow, OK?'

But he clearly wanted to tell us something before we went. He made several attempts, one word at a time.

'Music . . . has . . . charms . . . '

He sighed deeply, summoning up a huge effort, and the rest flew out on a surge of groaning words, 'to soothe . . . a savage breast.'

The effort was too great. For he lay still and spoke no more. In any case, our time was up; Sister's head came round the door and fixed us with an icy stare.

'Cheerio, Terry,' was all Mum could get out.

'Bye, Mr Wimbush,' I called.

In the corridor outside, Mum asked the inevitable, 'How is he?'

'Only doctor can say,' Sister replied. 'He's got third-degree burns covering about twenty per cent of his body. Poor fellow's still in shock. On top of that his lungs are clogged up with smoke. The next twenty-four hours are crucial. If he gets through that, he's likely to make it.'

'Thanks, Sister,' said Mum as we left.

Outside, in the fresh air, Mum stuck out her chin and breathed in deeply.

'Right,' she announced to the world, 'it's time to fight back.'

Tragedy

Mum's fight back started the very next day.

First she wrote to Winchester, informing the Arts Director of my 'accident'. Could they fit me in later? When she received no reply, she upped and went, dragging me along as 'Exhibit One', plaster, sling and all.

Poor Geo. K. Fry didn't know what hit him.

'Spoiling the boy's career . . . Deserves another chance . . . He'll be an eminent cellist one day . . . You'll be sorry . . . '

Patiently, he explained the rules and the orchestra's tight schedule. That didn't satisfy my mum. Oh no! She battered him until he offered a compromise.

'If your son is as promising as you claim—and *I'm* surely a better judge of that—he might get a place at the Winchester School of Music. I can arrange an interview if you wish.'

Mum's face fell.

'How much would it cost?' she said glumly.

'Oh, about fifteen thousand a year, not counting accessories.'

'I can't afford that,' she said simply, not even asking what 'accessories' were.

'Then, I'm sorry, madam,' he said with relief. 'Try again for the youth orchestra next year. Goodbye.'

That was that. No tutor. No music school. No youth orchestra. And, for the foreseeable future, no cello. That didn't suit Mum.

'Until your arm heals, you can practise music theory,' she ordered. 'I'll test you; when Terry's better he'll expect a progress report.'

Good old Mum. The cello finds work for idle hands. And my hands were even more idle now I'd lost my paper round.

'I can't use a one-handed paper boy,' argued Mr Gant.

Still, he did give me an extra week's wages and a box of chocolates for Mum. And that wasn't like stingy Mr Gant!

'You and I, son,' he said with a handshake, 'are too good for this estate.'

Mum and I visited Terry Wimbush every day. Sometimes we worked shifts: Mum day, me night. After a few days he was able to speak in short bursts and take in what was being said. I told him all the news.

'The place is getting back to normal. Even the hotheads are cooling down. No more marches. No more journalists—they've moved on to train crash victims and royal sex scandals.'

He wanted to know about my arm and the rehearsals. So I told all.

'The two Indian lads are due up in court next week. On charges of arson, attempted manslaughter, and GBH; the first two against you, the last against me. The family's had to move out of the area. Sad that, in a way. They weren't part of the riot. What they did was worse, though they probably see it as defending the family honour.'

I could tell from his reaction he was not so forgiving. So I changed the subject.

'As for Winchester, I'll try again next year. Me and Mum went to see the Arts Director. All he offered was an interview for a place at the music school. Silly prat! Where's Mum going to find that sort of dosh?'

In a hoarse whisper he said, 'Don't abandon the cello, Tom.'

'I won't, Mr Wimbush. Anyway, Mum wouldn't let me.'

119

When I left him that evening he still looked pretty awful: naked head criss-crossed with purple weals, nose and lips black and blue, cheeks grey-white like ash. Yet the burnt mask made his blue eyes stand out: bright, kind, hopeful.

His last words were, 'Don't forget my ticket . . . for your concert.'

I laughed. Yet on the walk home I called out to the seagulls circling overhead, 'I promise. One day.'

The phone rang next morning. It was so early I wasn't even up. Mum was slip-slopping around in the kitchen, giving Paddy his breakfast. I heard a muffled conversation; it didn't last long. Then I turned over and went back to sleep, relieved I didn't have to get up for papers.

When I woke up again, it was after nine. Although it was school holidays, I was surprised Mum hadn't shouted up the stairs. In fact, downstairs was uncommonly quiet: no music, no barking, no vacuum cleaner, no shake, rattle, and roll of breakfast things.

I cleaned my teeth and washed my face in the bathroom before creeping downstairs. At first I thought Mum had gone out. Yet I suddenly smelt cigarette smoke. Strange, she'd given up years ago, though she always kept a pack in the dresser drawer—'For Emergencies'.

What had made her light up?

I found her in the front room, still in her dressing gown. She was looking out of the front window, blue smoke was spiralling up through a bright shaft of sunbeams.

'Morning, Mum,' I said cheerily.

She was ominously silent. Mum wasn't prone to moods. So something big must have happened. Gran? Grandad? Uncle Bob had a dicky heart.

Best not to disturb her. I went into the kitchen, ruffled Paddy's fur and asked his advice while I poured cornflakes into a bowl. From his puzzled shrug, he didn't know either. Halfway through the cornflakes, Mum appeared in the doorway.

Thank goodness, she'd put out her cigarette, only half smoked.

'Terry's dead.'

No introduction. No explanation. Just 'Terry's dead.'

I froze, spoon halfway from bowl to mouth. Crazy thoughts clattered through my brain. But he can't be. He was on the mend. I only spoke to him last night. He was coming to my concert . . .

We were both struck dumb.

No doubt it would register later and we'd have a proper cry. But for the moment we couldn't utter a word.

Sozzled

At the crematorium it was just Mum, me, and Terry. Mum had seen to the funeral, buying a coffin and whatever bibs and bobs funerals needed. It made a whopping great hole in her savings; she even forked out for after-funeral fizzy wine, sausage rolls, and crisps back at our place.

There was quite a crowd. With all the joking and shouting you'd never think it was a party of mourners. Auntie Di brought Harriet; Gran and Grandad came. Terry's old English master was invited. Even a policewoman popped in, though when she saw the party she said she'd drop by later with some routine questions. On leaving, she said, 'This makes it murder!'

That set Grandad off, rabbiting on about 'mob frenzy' and 'innocent victims'. If anyone knew, they didn't mention a murder *motive*, which was just as well. Blame the mob.

And blame the mob they did. You wouldn't have thought these were the same people who'd shouted loudly for action, for hounding dirty old men off the estate, for 'outing' all homosexuals.

'He was such a nice, kindly man,' Auntie Di was saying. 'Always good for a laugh. If he were here now, he'd be telling one of his funny jokes and giggling away. Such a shame, innit.'

'If it weren't for them ignorant morons, he'd be here today,' added Uncle Bob with feeling. 'Whipping up a storm against innocent men like our Terry. I always liked him.'

Poor Harriet started to snivel in her grief—no doubt aided by a sneak at Gran's fizzy wine.

An awkward lull fell over the assembled company as Harriet's sobs set off Gran and Auntie Di. Heads turned to Mum as if expecting a speech. With half a sausage roll in one hand and an overflowing glass in the other, Mum stood up unsteadily in front of the fireplace. She was sozzled. But she was determined to have her say.

'Terry Wimbush was a queer,' she began loudly.

Oh my God! Here it comes! She'll tell them about me next . . .

In the shocked silence, she continued, 'He gave our Tom his *own* cello. He taught him all he knew. He was the kindest, funniest, cleverest man I ever knew.'

Heads nodded at this turn in Mum's speech.

'But he was a *queer*. And people poked fun at him, made jokes behind his back. Yes, Terry *was* always good for a laugh, all right. And when people got worked up after that little girl's murder, they looked for a scapegoat. Anyone would do. Someone different. *Any old queer!* Isn't that right?'

She swayed forward and Auntie Di caught her before she fell, helping her to an armchair.

'Now, now, Jeanette,' she murmured soothingly. 'Don't upset yourself, love. Come on, sit down and take it easy.'

To cover the embarrassed silence, Uncle Bob, no doubt calling on his DJ experience, suggested a song. Without waiting for general consent, he began, 'For he's a jolly good fellow, for he's a jolly good fellow . . . '

Waving his arms about as if conducting a choir, he got the party to join in.

'For he's a jolly good fe-e-llow. And so say all of us!'

I couldn't help wondering what Terry Wimbush made of it, looking down from on high.

123

'Pardon me,' came a voice beside me. 'I must be going.'

It was Mr 'Scratch', the schoolmaster.

'Oh, I forgot to tell you,' I said. 'I gave him your message. It must have meant something. For the first word he spoke in hospital was something about . . . uh, what was it? ''Concave''?'

'Congreve. William Congreve.'

He sighed sadly.

'Once a scholar, always a scholar. Congreve's an English poet and dramatist, friend of Jonathan Swift, of *Gulliver's Travels* fame. That quotation always tickled Terry because of all his spurned female admirers.'

He turned to go.

'Hold on, Mr . . . ,' I said, forgetting his name. 'Terry Wimbush said something else. I haven't forgotten it: ''Music has charms to soothe a savage beast''.'

'Breast, *not* beast!' he said. 'That's Congreve too. I think Terry meant that for you, sonny.'

With that he was gone. His place was taken by a totally unexpected visitor. As the old man limped down the road, he passed a stocky, spiky-haired woman coming our way. Surely not! I stood holding the door open, like a sentry at his post. Stop! Who goes there? Friend or Foe?

This was definitely 'Foe'.

'Hiya, Tom,' she said, unsure of herself. 'Mum in?'

'She's not well,' I lied, barring the way.

She must have heard the hubbub in our front room because she muttered, 'You got company. I'll come back another time.'

Just as she was going, Auntie Di pushed past and called her back, 'Come on in, come in. The more the merrier.'

The wine must have addled her brain. What did she think Mum's reaction would be on this day of all days?

The appearance of Tracy stopped all chatter. Luckily, Mum wasn't in a fit state to throw her out.

Tight-lipped and pale, the rebel leader stood, arms folded, in front of Mum. 'Look, Jeanette, I've come to say sorry, see. I didn't want this. But I ain't no coward; it weren't easy to come. That's all I got to say. Sorry, gal.'

She turned on her heel, went out of the door and clip-clopped down the street.

For the first time that day Mum had a little cry.

Terry's Will

A few days later Mum had to go into town to 'tie up loose ends' at some solicitor's. She was gone a couple of hours. Since she'd threatened a music test on her return, I got busy swotting up on note-reading and theory. I'd reached a stage where I could play tunes in my head, pressing the strings with my left hand.

It seemed to come naturally, like my goalkeeping, only more so. Not at all like art or maths or French where I was *naturally* a dimhead.

I heard the front door open and shut. Almost at once, Mum's voice rang out, 'Come down here at once!'

Charming. Smack in the middle of an exercise. That wasn't like Mum. She didn't demand instant attention. Perhaps she'd brought back some hot fish and chips. No such luck. She was sitting at the kitchen table, scanning a long sheet of paper. Peering over her shoulder, I noticed a stamp at the bottom and old-fashioned writing on creamy-coloured art paper.

'This, Tom, is a Will,' declared Mum. 'Terry's Will.'

'Don't tell me,' I said. 'He won the Lottery and left it all to you.'

'Not exactly,' she responded slowly. 'He has left his *house* to you, though. It's worth about sixty or seventy grand.'

I didn't understand.

'But I want to live here with you, Mum.'

'No, idiot, the sale of his house will bring in money to pay for music school. *If* you're bright enough to get in!'

It took a while to sink in. But Mum was already

making plans. Right away she telephoned Winchester and fixed an appointment for the following Monday.

'But I can't play,' I objected, suddenly getting cold feet. 'It'll be another couple of months before my arm's strong enough.'

'You've got two arms, haven't you? The man says he wants to see your finger technique. Mr Fry has put in a good word for you, so you can't let him down.'

'But, Mum . . . I can't live without you . . . '

'You'll come home at weekends.'

'But, Mum, they're all snobs, rich kids; I'd hate it . . . '

'You'll get used to it. Don't grow like them, that's all.'

'My football'll suffer . . . '

'Why?'

I had no answer to that. So I gave her the clincher. 'What if they find out I'm gay?'

'So what? What if your mates here find out? What if the neighbours find out? What if our family finds out? What if the world finds out? Sooner or later you'll have to decide: live your life in the closet or stand up and be proud of what you are. It's your choice.'

Oh yeah. It was all right for her. She was one of the great majority. She swam with the tide. I was fighting against it. But what finally made up my mind was what she'd once said: *Let people judge you on what you can do. Not what you are.*

What I could do was play the cello, make music, good music. I didn't boast about it, even to Mum. But I *knew* I was good. I felt it with my whole body, as Terry Wimbush had once said on the train. Of course, I had to practise, practise, practise. I had to learn from others. I needed a good teacher with Terry gone. That's what music school could give.

Anyway, there was another reason. I *owed* it to Terry Wimbush at least to give it a go. And if I did get in, I'd give it my best shot. For his sake.

Another Audition

As she told me many times, Mum wasn't going to live her life through me. 'Get a life,' she was often saying. And now she was keen to show me *she'd* got a life by 'taking steps'.

To her the 'steps' were all part of the 'fight back'. Terry's death had made her all the more determined to do something with her life.

She started by writing a long letter to *The News*, saying how the estate wasn't home to bigots and dupes of the gutter press, how cynical rich journalists had used her and others to sensationalize serious issues. Most residents were decent people who hated prejudice of all kinds.

She, Mum, was setting up a new RAP—Residents Against Prejudice—that would last for years, not days; it was based on education, not ignorance, on toleration, not violence.

As a start, she wrote, the local school was letting her use a small wing for the new 'Terry Wimbush' RAP Centre. She'd persuaded the Portsmouth Football Club captain, a black player, to come to talk about 'Racism in Football'. Other meetings would follow.

She ended by saying she didn't expect the paper to publish her letter since it was 'from an ordinary housewife saying ordinary things'.

To her surprise, her letter *was* published, on Saturday too. Not only that, at the bottom of the Readers' Letters column was the 'cuddly' picture of Mum and me.

Monday morning, all spruced up, clean white sling washed and ironed, I was standing in a studio of the music school. Mum had lugged my cello all the way from the station; she was now fussing about with the fold-away stand. Every squeak and cough echoed round the walls of the vast empty room.

The staff must have turned out in force because on one side of a long green baize table sat five tutors. The smarmy, unsmiling one in the centre clapped even before I'd twitched a finger.

'Madam,' he addressed Mum, 'will you wait outside, please?'

She was a bit miffed at that.

When the door closed, he turned on me.

'Play!'

Play? Couldn't he see? My bowing arm was in a solid cast held up by a cloth sling. I wanted to run away, but my feet were rooted to the floor. The man frowned. Clearly, I hadn't understood English.

'Play!' he repeated, more loudly this time. 'Sing or hum the tune as you play with your left hand.'

Oh! How odd.

'Ave M-Maria,' I stuttered in my still squeaky voice.

This was madness. Still, Schubert had written it as a song. If only I knew the words!

I wedged the cello between my knees, flexed the fingers of my left hand, and started playing. My head replaced my bowing arm. As I 'played'—pressing the instrument's neck and singing—I forgot all about the audience of five; I was carried away by the music.

I was under the lofty white dome of a cathedral, a great choir was singing 'Ave Maria! Ave Maria!', then dum-dum-dumming to words they'd forgotten. The music floated up through the air on angels' wings, fluttering before a marble statue of Mary, Mother of God, then soaring up to serenade the glorious murals round the dome.

130

'Stop!'

A shout shattered the image. Instead of angels I saw five faces staring at me. A haughty voice came out of a female figure at the end of the row.

'Why do you want to play the cello?'

She caught me on the hop. Why *did* I want to play? Because Mum had once played the flute. Because Terry Wimbush had given me lessons. Because I'd won the school music prize.

'Dunno,' I offered.

By the look on her face I could see my music education going down the pan. Think, Tom, think. Why? Why?

'My mum took me to a concert once,' I began. 'Elgar's Cello Concerto. And I felt the music. Not here, in my head, but in my heart. It just took control of me. It made me cry. I'd never felt like that before . . . '

'I see,' said the woman with a superior smile.

She didn't seem convinced.

'Anything you want to add?' said smarmy face in the middle.

'No,' I mumbled, getting up to go.

I was just about to step towards the door when I suddenly turned back.

'Yes, there is,' I said firmly. 'See, on the estate where I live, playing the cello's seen as, well, you wouldn't understand, a bit cissy. I got my arm broken because of it. Even if *you* don't take me on, it won't stop me playing. I'm going to learn to play *really* well, make my kind of people listen—so they can enjoy beautiful music as well.'

I'd stopped speaking, yet no one said anything for several moments. Finally, the man in the centre coughed and said, 'Uh, thank you, Goodall. That will be all. Wait outside, if you please.'

131

Twenty Years Old

Looking back, it seems as if there were two Toms. One left school and joined his mates working as a fitter or coppersmith in the dockyard. The other flew away on a magic carpet to a wonderful land of adventure. Don't think the reality was all floating on air. The first few nights were the worst. Sharing a room with five other boys really freaked me out. I cried for Mum under the bed covers.

Nor did I get on with the others at first: they were always poking fun at the way I talked and other 'bad' habits—like the way I ate my soup or called the loo 'toilet' instead of 'lavatory'.

But I learned the hard way and eventually settled in. What saw me through was my music. Not only did I learn a lot about the cello, I played in small groups—trio, quartet, quintet—where each instrument supported the other. The result was great music-making.

Soon I came to realize the simple truth that respect *had to be earned*, by showing others I was as good as them. Different maybe, but just as good in my own way. I often recalled Terry's words—*'Music has charms to soothe a savage breast'*. My playing almost always worked its magic, massaging away the pain and sadness of my personal life.

When I first went to the school I thought I would never match the other kids. Some had started to play at three or four! Imagine that! Their parents had forced them to practise a couple of hours a day. And they were so sure of themselves, even too sure, laughing at my bowing technique and the way I jammed the cello between my legs—'Like a nutcracker,' one toffee-nosed boy said. My tutors didn't try to alter my playing—'Too late for that,' they decided.

Yet after a few months I saw I had a big advantage over these confident musicians. I possessed something they didn't: *dedication*. Where they practised three hours a day, I practised five. Where they chilled out with horror books and teenage mags, I studied theory and the biographies of famous composers—sort of making up for lost time. For me music was almost life itself.

No one scoffed any more. Some actually began to seek *my* company, *my* advice, *my* help. I even persuaded my string quartet friends to put on a performance at Mum's 'Terry Wimbush RAP Centre'. Not in the black 'Mickey Mouse' suits and bow ties we sometimes wore, but in casual gear—jeans and sweaters.

Mum's Centre had never witnessed chamber music before. And although it was a foul night, a good thirty people turned out—*and* they seemed to enjoy themselves. It was as unusual an experience for the Winchester musicians as it was for local residents.

Both sides benefited. None more so than Mum, who kept going on about how her 'little boy had got on'. Dear Mum, what with social work no one could say she was living her life through me. But her beaming face betrayed her enormous pride.

Mum was right. Her Centre did last for years. Its popularity grew and grew, with folk music, quiz and poetry evenings, art displays, talks on anything from 'The Blitz' to 'Being Gay'.

And would you believe it? Who should turn up to the 'gay' night but Sanjeev! He came with his partner—a fitness instructor like himself. It was the first time Mum had clapped eyes on him since the 'incident'. He'd brought Mum a present: a keep-fit video and book on yoga. That was by way of an apology for the attack on me (his brothers had been sent to prison for manslaughter for their attack on Terry). Sanjeev didn't even ask after me. Sad, that.

So here I was, about to make my concert debut. On my twentieth birthday. By coincidence, I was playing the Elgar Cello Concerto with the Bournemouth Symphony Orchestra. And at Portsmouth Guildhall! I'd already completed school and made music my career. For two years I'd been playing in local groups and orchestras and doing the odd solo in competitions.

At last a professional orchestra had invited me to play with them. A cello concerto all on my own.

This was it. Make or break time. If I did well, I might become a concert cellist, travelling the world. If I flopped, it was back to playing 'second fiddle' among the other cellos. What made me all the more nervous was that Mum had bought up tickets for the first three rows—'For friends and relatives,' she said.

She didn't have enough friends and relatives to fill half a row, let alone three! I was fully expecting to play to a half-empty house!

I couldn't bring myself to venture out of the dressing room in the first half of the concert. I sat alone, shaking like a leaf and feeling sick. I had no idea what to expect when I walked on stage for the start of the second half of the programme. As it was, my entry was greeted by some polite applause . . . and cheers and whistles! Not at all the reception I was used to. For the first time I stole a glance at the auditorium.

I could hardly believe my eyes!

Half the estate must have been there, whistling and stamping. They not only filled the front three rows, they were all over the place—in the middle and at the back of the stalls, upstairs in the circle, down the sides.

They obviously weren't used to concert halls . . .

Mum was sitting in the centre of the front row, wearing her black concert dress with a double string of pearls—she looked very beautiful. On one side were Auntie Di, Uncle Bob, and Harriet, on the other was an empty seat.

A lump came to my throat. He'd so wanted a ticket for my concert. I could see him now, shushing the rough and rowdy, his ruddy face tilted to one side, totally absorbed in the music, *my music*.

The conductor held up his hand for silence.

'Ladies and gentlemen, this evening is a special occasion. Mr Tom Goodall is making his concert debut. He is to play the Elgar Cello Concerto in E minor, Opus 85.'

Suddenly silence. You could have heard a pin drop.

'This is for you, Mum,' I said under my breath.

The conductor held up his baton and swept the orchestra with a severe look, demanding instant attention. His glare finally fell on me—and he gave a big saucy wink! Once the music began, my nerves miraculously melted away. I lived every note, every phrase, every emotion.

It was only when the last note had died away that I came back to earth. My head was bathed in sweat, my hands tingled, my body felt like a wrung-out rag. Yet I was so elated.

After a moment's hush, the hall exploded with noise: clapping, shouting, whistling, stamping. Cries of *'Bravo! Bravo!'* swept over the waves of applause. The front three rows were on their feet, hands in the air, reaching out to congratulate me.

Now a new sound came up from the audience: 'More! Encore!' It accompanied me all the way from stage to wings and back, as I reappeared to take a bow.

135

Finally, after the third bow, the conductor tapped the stand with his baton and waved me back to my seat.

'What's it to be, Tom?' he whispered. 'Go on, announce it yourself.'

I coughed, looked at Mum and smiled. Then I said in a low, husky voice, 'Lennon and McCartney, "Yesterday".'

And I played. For him.